W9-AGP-432

"What can I do for you?"

Her eyes darkened to a shade of hunter green. "You can tell me what my dead husband's brother has to do with you and your children."

He felt like he'd been sucker punched. "What are you talking about?"

"The rumor is that Billy Bob Adams is the one suing you for custody of the girls.... Is it true?"

She wasn't going to let it drop. She was going to force him to tell her something that would rock her world.

He let out a long breath. "Okay. You want it straight?"

"That's what I just said. Why would my dead husband's brother sue for custody of your children?"

"Because he's their uncle, Jen. Your dead husband is the twins' biological father."

Dear Reader,

Brr... February's below-freezing temperatures call for a mug of hot chocolate, a fuzzy afghan and a heartwarming book from Silhouette Romance. Our books will heat you to the tips of your toes with the sizzling sexual tension that courses between our stubborn heroes and the determined heroines who ultimately melt their hardened hearts.

In Judy Christenberry's *Least Likely To Wed*, her sinfully sexy cowboy hero has his plans for lifelong bachelorhood foiled by the searing kisses of a spirited single mom. While in Sue Swift's *The Ranger & the Rescue*, an amnesiac cowboy stakes a claim on the heart of a flame-haired heroine—but will the fires of passion still burn when he regains his memory?

Tensions reach the boiling point in Raye Morgan's *She's Having My Baby!*—the final installment of the miniseries HAVING THE BOSS'S BABY—when our heroine discovers just who fathered her baby-to-be.... And tempers flare in Rebecca Russell's *Right Where He Belongs*, in which our handsome hero must choose between his cold plan for revenge and a woman's warm and tender love.

Then simmer down with the incredibly romantic heroes in Teresa Southwick's *What If We Fall In Love?* and Colleen Faulkner's *A Shocking Request*. You'll laugh, you'll cry, you'll fall in love all over again with these deeply touching stories about widowers who get a second chance at love.

So this February, come in from the cold and warm your heart and spirit with one of these temperature-raising books from Silhouette Romance. Don't forget the marshmallows!

Happy reading!

Mary-Theresa Hussey

Mary-Theresa Hussey
Senior Editor

Please address questions and book requests to:
Silhouette Reader Service
U.S.: 3010 Walden Ave., P.O. Box 1325, Buffalo, NY 14269
Canadian: P.O. Box 609, Fort Erie, Ont. L2A 5X3

What If We Fall in Love?

TERESA SOUTHWICK

SILHOUETTE *Romance*®

Published by Silhouette Books

America's Publisher of Contemporary Romance

If you purchased this book without a cover you should be aware
that this book is stolen property. It was reported as "unsold and
destroyed" to the publisher, and neither the author nor the
publisher has received any payment for this "stripped book."

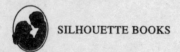

SILHOUETTE BOOKS

ISBN 0-373-19572-9

WHAT IF WE FALL IN LOVE?

Copyright © 2002 by Teresa Ann Southwick

All rights reserved. Except for use in any review, the reproduction
or utilization of this work in whole or in part in any form by any
electronic, mechanical or other means, now known or hereafter
invented, including xerography, photocopying and recording, or in
any information storage or retrieval system, is forbidden without
the written permission of the editorial office, Silhouette Books,
300 East 42nd Street, New York, NY 10017 U.S.A.

All characters in this book have no existence outside the imagination of
the author and have no relation whatsoever to anyone bearing the same
name or names. They are not even distantly inspired by any individual
known or unknown to the author, and all incidents are pure invention.

This edition published by arrangement with Harlequin Books S.A.

® and TM are trademarks of Harlequin Books S.A., used under license.
Trademarks indicated with ® are registered in the United States Patent
and Trademark Office, the Canadian Trade Marks Office and in other
countries.

Visit Silhouette at www.eHarlequin.com

Printed in U.S.A.

Books by Teresa Southwick

TERESA SOUTHWICK

is a native Californian who has been transplanted to Texas. Having lived with her husband of twenty-five-plus years and two handsome sons, she has been surrounded by heroes for a long time. Reading has been her passion since she was a girl. She couldn't be more delighted that her dream of writing full-time has come true. Her favorite things include: holding a baby, the fragrance of jasmine, walks on the beach, the patter of rain on the roof and, above all, happy endings.

Teresa has also written historical romance novels under the same name.

OKLAHOMA

NEW
MEXICO

ARK.

* Grady's Ranch   ★ Dallas

● Destiny

LA.

TEXAS

N

MEXICO

Gulf of
Mexico

All underlined places are fictitious.

MAIN STREET, DESTINY

Charlie's
Tractor Supply —
Where
Texas Ranchers
Shop

Road
Kill
Café

This
'n
That
(Maggie Benson,
Owner)

Law Office
Jensen Stevens,
Attorney

Doc Holloway's
Office

Sheriff
Grady O'Connor's
Office

It's Geek
to Me—
Computer
Equipment
(Jack Riley, Owner)

Chapter One

There was something about a man in uniform. And Sheriff Grady O'Connor was definitely something.

Jensen Stevens didn't expect to notice. She couldn't remember the last time a good-looking guy had gotten her attention. But as the sheriff moseyed up the bleacher stairs at the north Texas high school rodeo championships, she couldn't take her eyes off him. After years in suspended animation her feminine radar suddenly switched on to signal a hunk at four o'clock.

Grady was a local rancher as well as Destiny's acting sheriff. It was disconcerting that once he'd snagged her attention, she couldn't seem to disengage. She wondered if he looked as good in cowboy duds as he did in his lawman ensemble. His short-sleeved tan shirt and matching khaki pants with the brown-and-beige stripe down the leg suited him to a T. No doubt about it—he was walking, talking hero material.

This was only the second time she could remember

her heart skipping a beat at the sight of a man. The first was a decade ago and she'd married him.

"Hello, Counselor." Grady sat his long, lanky self down beside her.

"Hello, Sheriff." A loud crackling came over the public address system. "Sounds like they're having trouble with the mike."

"Yeah."

He removed his dark brown Stetson and ran splayed fingers through his short, military-style brown hair. After propping his boot on the bench in front of him, he rested his forearm on a thickly muscled thigh and tapped his hat against his leg. His uniform looked freshly pressed, in spite of the evening heat and humidity typical of Texas in June. The shirt hugged the contours of his impressive chest and detailed his attention-getting physique. Reflector aviator sunglasses were tucked into one of his pockets.

"Long time no see," she said.

"Not that long. I saw you four days ago. On the first day of the championships when you rolled back into Destiny in that sweet BMW convertible."

"Okay. But not since then." At least, not close enough to stake out her comfort zone. Like now. She'd only seen him from a distance, taking care of rodeo security.

In high school they'd hung out in the same group of kids who rodeoed. Then life intervened and they'd gone their separate ways. Since they'd reacquainted several days before, she hadn't really thought about him. Apparently distance was her friend. Because now she couldn't help thinking he was like an allergic reaction. The first exposure had produced a mild warning. The second—watch out.

Grady was not hard on her eyes with his well-shaped nose, nice mouth, soft-looking lips not too thin or too thick. His jaw was square and rugged the way a guy's jaw should be. He was a man who would turn female heads wherever he went. The rodeo was being held on her sister's ranch and Jensen had been a spectator every night since arriving. She was grateful that, until now, she hadn't spectated much of the sexy sheriff.

"Are you enjoying yourself?" he asked.

"Yeah. I like watching," She cleared her throat. "It's fun to observe the high school kids interact with each other. I can't believe I was ever that age."

"Right. You're practically ready for assisted living at Leisure Village."

She laughed, then smoothed her palms over the skirt of her floral cotton sundress that didn't come close to covering her knees. When she saw him glance in that direction, she very much wished she'd worn jeans and boots.

"You know what I mean."

"Yeah," he said.

She looked back at the arena where the John Deere tractor was smoothing the dirt for the last three events of the championships.

"I do get nervous for the competitors," she admitted. "I heard an announcement that sounded like Mitch Rafferty was going to hold a spur-of-the-moment bull-riding seminar," she said, feeling a knot of anxiety tighten inside her.

"I heard it, too. That event *is* coming up."

Jensen met his laserlike blue gaze and knew he was warning her. And she knew why. "Ten years ago tonight Zach won the event.'' Then he'd asked her to run away with him and get married.

"Yeah, how could I forget.''

She'd agreed and followed the professional rodeo circuit with the man she had loved. They'd had one year together. Then he'd taken a kick to the head and been killed instantly at a rodeo in Las Vegas.

The following nine years had been profoundly painful. Only work had helped. College classes and then law school had taken the edge off her acute loneliness. Now she just had her memories, and that was enough. She wouldn't take another chance. She would never hurt like that again.

Grady rubbed his index finger over the crown of his hat. "After intermission there's pole bending then barrel racing. Last is bull-riding,'' he said, studying her intently. "Mitch was national champion. He's a good one to give the kids pointers—to avoid mistakes that could cause injuries.''

Lord, she hoped that wasn't pity she saw in Grady's eyes. She didn't need anyone to feel sorry for her. Life was a series of trade-offs. She'd lost the love of her life, but she had a career as a family law attorney, even if she would never have a family of her own.

"I haven't been to the rodeo since Zach died,'' she admitted, not sure why she was sharing that piece of information with him.

"Why now?''

"Good question.'' She stared into the distance. "Probably motive and opportunity. I've been too busy to go out of my way. And I guess I just didn't want to.''

"Why didn't you keep his last name?''

"Adams?'' She looked at him and thought for a

moment. "I'm not sure. Maybe because we were only married a year. Maybe because my folks didn't approve of us running off. Maybe because I never changed any of my legal documents."

Because they'd traveled to rodeos all over the country, she'd never bothered to change her name on her driver's license or with the social security department. And then she'd lost him. It was too late.

"How long has it been since you've been back to Destiny?" he asked.

"About six months. I was here for the holidays."

"I didn't know that."

"It seems I never run into you on my visits home. I guess Kasey and Stacey and the ranch keep you pretty busy."

"Those girls could use a full-time bodyguard," he agreed. "But the fact that I haven't seen you, at least in a professional capacity, is good news. That means I never had to run you in for disturbing the peace."

He grinned suddenly and she was grateful to be sitting down. The humor transformed his face, chasing away the frown lines and seriousness. Oh, my. Cool, calm and detached, he was attractive enough to earn the attention of card-carrying man haters. But the amused expression he wore now made him downright devastatingly gorgeous.

She swallowed the sudden thickness in her throat. "As an officer of the court, getting arrested for anything wouldn't be good."

"True enough. So how do you like being back? What do you think of the changes Taylor's made on the Circle S?"

Question number one translated: Do you still have feelings for Mitch Rafferty, the guy you dumped be-

fore marrying Zach? Subtext of question number two:
Do you resent the fact that your little sister has turned
the family ranch into a Texas-style bed-and-breakfast?

She decided to ignore number one and go to question two. "I'm so proud of Taylor I could just bust.
She's done a terrific job. There's no doubt in my mind
that the dude ranch will be very successful for her."

After their father's death from a heart attack, her
younger sister had taken on a mortgage to buy out
Jensen and their mother, financing her retirement to
Dallas. To pad her profit margin in case of natural
disasters or a drop in beef prices, Taylor had followed
her dream of taking in guests to show them the joy
and excitement of the Western lifestyle. Based on advance reservations, she was going to be wildly successful.

"What about Mitch?" Grady's eyes held a gleam
of interest.

Jensen wanted to forget how young and stupid she'd
been when she'd selfishly hurt Mitch. But he and
Mitch were friends. Of course he would care.

"We talked the day I arrived and worked everything
out. I apologized for my youthful stupidity and he graciously accepted. Then I gave him my blessing to
court Taylor and welcomed him to the family."

"Why?"

"Does the word *duh* mean anything to you, Sheriff?
I think your powers of deduction need some fine-tuning."

"Could you be more specific?"

"Mitch is in love with Taylor."

"No…"

"He always has been."

"I don't believe it."

"Cross my heart," she said, doing just that. "I know what I'm talking about. He had a chip on his shoulder when we dated, but he could always talk to my sister. I think they've had a thing for each other since way back when. If I hadn't handled things so badly all those years ago, he might not have left town. The two of them would have gotten together a lot sooner."

"They're not together now—"

A loud crackling noise over the public address system interrupted him. Then the weirdly echoing sound of an obviously open microphone filled the stands.

"I love you, Mitch."

Jensen raised an eyebrow. She couldn't see the two, but she recognized her sister's voice.

"Now the damn mike works." The voice was definitely Mitch's and more than a little exasperated. Then there was a click and the PA system was shut off.

Jensen couldn't resist flashing a smug smile at Grady. "That was Taylor and I rest my case."

"You win, Counselor."

She wouldn't call herself a winner—especially in love. But she couldn't be happier that Taylor had finally declared her feelings for Mitch. It was way past time for her to get it right with the man she'd loved since she was fourteen years old.

Grady studied the beautiful woman to his right. Jensen Stevens was a male fantasy in a floral cotton sundress. She was a tiny little thing, five foot two if she was an inch. Her red-highlighted brown hair tickled her shoulders with every lively movement of her head. Big, expressive green eyes regarded him in a completely self-satisfied way and for the life of him he couldn't work up the will to care.

Grady followed her gaze as it shifted. She was looking down at Mitch and Taylor, who were strolling off by themselves, talking earnestly, with their arms around each other's waists as they stared deeply into one another's eyes.

"They win," she said wistfully.

"I guess so."

If Jen was right, Mitch and Taylor had been in love for a long time. Grady hoped his friends would find couple happiness, even if he didn't believe it existed. He'd never experienced the emotion himself.

"I saw your twins earlier. Kasey and Stacey are completely adorable. You must be very proud of them."

He thought about his girls, and a warm feeling filled him. They were his life. So he stood corrected. He knew deep-down, put-your-life-on-the-line love, just not the romantic kind.

"Yeah. I think I'll keep them around."

"You may be peeling them off the ceiling tonight." Jensen clasped her fingers together in her lap.

"Why?"

"I fed them cotton candy, red punch, red vines and red hots."

"You have the right to remain silent. If you give up that right, I'll know who to blame. You fed them sugar and red stuff at the same time?"

"Guilty as charged."

"Why?"

She shrugged. "Because they wanted it."

"Do I need to read you your rights before I run you in?"

"On what charge?"

"Contributing to the hyperactivity of minors." He snapped his fingers. "I believe in making the punishment fit the crime. Why don't you come over and help me put them to bed?"

"Ooh. You are devious," she said. "The perfect father for future teenage twins." Her teasing look faded and was replaced by pensive. "How do you do it?"

"What?"

"Raise them alone. You must miss Lacey."

Lacey Miller O'Connor. His wife. She'd died right after the twins were born—complications of childbirth. He rested his other boot on the metal bleacher seat, then twirled his hat in his hands.

He thought about how to respond. "She was my best friend." That didn't exactly answer the question, but it was all he wanted to share with her.

"Didn't you live with her family for a while?"

He nodded. "They took me in after my folks died."

"Car accident, wasn't it?"

"Yeah."

"It must have been devastating for you. I can't even imagine what that must have been like. But you and Lacey?" She smiled. "Friendship, love, then marriage."

"We hardly had time to know what being married meant."

"If anybody knows what that feels like, it's me," she said. "I often wished that Zach and I had had a child together. At least you have your girls."

"Yeah."

And that was his secret, he thought.

"Have you considered marrying again?" she asked.

"You applying for the position?"

Why had he said that? Deflect the question? Put a stop to personal questions? Or was there a deeper, more wishful reason?

Her green eyes widened and she tugged at the hem of her cotton skirt. "Objection," she said, as if she were addressing the court.

"Overruled. Are you interested in the job?"

"Job? So marriage to you would be a chore? A duty? An assignment?"

"Heck, no. I'm a swell guy."

"Then why haven't you remarried?" She zeroed that green-eyed gaze on him. "And don't tell me no one's been interested."

One corner of his mouth rose. "Is that a compliment?"

"Are you fishing for one?"

"Always."

"Okay. Let me shoot your ego full of steroids. You're a nice-looking man."

"Nice-looking? That's the best you can do?"

The glaring spotlights overhead clearly showed the blush that crept into her cheeks. For the life of him, he couldn't seem to let her off the hook. He was deliberately baiting her.

"Words are my life, Sheriff. And no, that's not the best I can do. However, it's all I'm willing to say. But my point is, and I do have one, that women must notice you. Is there a problem?"

"Yeah. Two. Their names are Kasey and Stacey."

"What do the twins have to do with it?"

"Everything. Either I meet someone they like who would be a good mother to them but doesn't do a thing for me, or I find a woman I like and they make gagging noises when I mention her name.''

"Gagging noises? Those sweet angels I saw just a little while ago?''

"Angels?'' He put the palm of his hand to her forehead, as if to check for fever. A teasing gesture. Not meant to be more. But the arc of electricity the touch produced put a lie to that and he quickly pulled back. "Those two could make a career out of duping innocent folks. Their favorite trick is switching identities. Most people can't tell them apart.''

"Yes, angels. They gave me the cheat sheet.''

"The what?''

"The cheat sheet for who's who.''

"They must like you.''

"Of course they do. I plied them with red vines, red hots and red punch. What's not to like? Besides, all that red dye works better than truth serum.''

He shook his head. "I still say they must like you. I can't get them to cooperate after that much junk. Mostly they're devils disguised as angels.''

"Those girls are beautiful little cherubs.'' She grinned, showing straight, even teeth and a beautiful smile that made her green eyes sparkle like precious gems.

"Okay. Eighty percent of the time they're as good as gold. But they have their dark side.''

"No,'' she said, exaggerating the word.

"Everyone does, Jen.''

He wasn't thinking of the twins now, but her husband. He wasn't the man she'd thought. But there was no reason to speak ill of the dead, and worse, destroy her illusions. And she did have them, or she wouldn't have stayed single all this time mourning the creep.

"I know that, Grady. I'm not naive," she scoffed. "In my line of work, I see the best and worst."

"I suppose that's true. So do I."

"Tell me again why you haven't remarried?"

"You're like a dog with a favorite bone on that subject."

Her eyes widened. "Geez, I'm sorry. I guess questions are what I do. But I don't usually badger my friends. Really I don't. Maybe I'm a little tense. Because of the next couple of events. Maybe I should go..."

He put his hand on her arm. "No. I don't mind distracting you. I guess I haven't remarried because I can't find someone I like."

"We've already established that hordes of women are on your trail. Aren't you just a tad picky?"

"*We* haven't established anything. And if the counselor would let me finish my thought..."

"By all means," she said, with an expansive hand gesture that told him he had the floor.

"*If* I was looking, it would be for a woman I was attracted to who would also be a good mother to the girls."

She tapped her lip with her index finger. "If? You're not looking?"

"That would be a waste of time and energy."

"Why?"

"Because it doesn't exist."

"It? You mean love? Relationships?"

"Either or both—yes."

"Hmm."

He looked at her. "What does that mean?"

"Just that you're very cynical. I've heard that men

who love once are likely to find it again. So why would you think it doesn't exist? You loved Lacey.''

And there was another secret he would keep. ''Has anyone ever mentioned that you ask a lot of questions?''

''Yes.''

''I guess that goes with the territory. Being a lawyer and all.''

''I guess.''

''So what's *your* story? Why isn't a pretty lady like you married by now with a couple of kids?''

When her sunny expression faded, Grady could have kicked himself from here to kingdom come. He'd only wanted to sidestep her questions, not take the smile from her face.

''I already had my chance at love.''

''So women get just one chance? It's only men who are likely to find it again?''

She shrugged. ''I had one perfect year with the love of my life. I won't ever find that again and, like you just said, looking is a waste of time and energy that could be put to better use.''

Grady wished he could tell her the truth, because the man she'd loved hadn't been worth the time and energy she'd wasted on him. Along with Mitch, Dev Hart and Jack Riley, he'd spent a lot of years keeping the hurtful information from her. If she learned the facts, what would be the point? It wasn't only Zach's memory that was keeping her single. Jensen had been busy with college, law school and pursuing her career. She was made for love, and when the time was right it would find her—whether or not she knew the ugly truth about the jerk she'd married.

Right now Grady had better things to do. Like putting the stars back in her eyes. "Okay. So let me see if I've got this straight. You're a do-as-I-say-not-as-I-do kind of gal?"

"Of course not." Her gaze narrowed on him.

No stars yet, Grady noted, but the shadows were gone. "But you think I should marry again, and it's not in the cards for you?"

"You have two girls who need a mother. I just have me," she pointed out.

"All the more reason you should be a touch more open-minded about finding someone. I'm not alone."

She lifted her chin slightly. "Being alone is nothing to be ashamed of. I happen to like my own companionship. The company is always agreeable—quite witty and stimulating, in fact," she said, her eyes twinkling.

Almost there, he noted. But he wouldn't let up until he coaxed a smile from her. "I'd like to try that sometime."

"Being alone?" she asked.

"Considering Kasey and Stacey are nine and talk like a couple of magpies, being alone sounds like a small slice of heaven. But that's not what I meant."

It looked as if she was struggling to hold back a laugh as she caught the corner of her lip between her teeth. "Then what did you mean?"

"You said you like being alone. I'd like to be alone with you, too."

Eyes wide, she stared at him for several moments. Son of a gun, he'd rendered the legal eagle speechless. Not a bad night's work. On top of that, he'd made her smile, or would have if she'd just let go. And the stars were definitely back in her eyes, along with a blush on her cheeks.

Before he could figure out what to say next, a busty, dark-haired, approximately thirty-year-old woman stopped on the bleacher stair beside him. "Sheriff O'Connor?" she asked.

"Yes, ma'am," he said, putting on his hat as he stood. "What can I do for you?"

She pulled an envelope from the large denim bag slung over her shoulder and handed it to him, then started back down the bleachers. She looked back and said, "You've just been served."

Chapter Two

As Grady studied the summons, Jensen named every emotion that washed over his face—surprise, shock, anger, then fear. She swore he turned white beneath his tan. Standing, she put a hand on his arm.

"What is it?" she asked.

"Nothing." He quickly folded the papers and shoved them back in the envelope, then tucked the packet into his shirt pocket.

"I'm a lawyer, Grady. Someone else might buy that it's nothing, but I know better. You're being sued. What I want to know is by whom and what for?"

"It's just a pain-in-the-neck suit. No big deal."

"If you tell me not to worry my pretty little head…"

"Would I do that?" He smiled, but it was strained.

She knew this, even though they hadn't seen each other much in the past ten years. But they'd been friends once; she didn't believe he'd changed all that much. So two things were clear to her—he was shook. And he wouldn't admit it. Why?

It was obvious—he was a man. A lawman. It all boiled down to testosterone and training.

"I'd be happy to read the papers and advise you," she offered. "You can't turn down free legal advice."

"Watch me. Thanks, but no thanks." He snapped out the words like pistol shots, sharp and shocking.

Before she cross-examined him, common sense prevailed. It was none of her business. She'd offered help and he'd turned her down. End of story.

"I have to find the girls," he said quickly, and there was a hint of desperation in his voice. "I need to get them home."

"Yeah, it's getting late."

Before he could answer, there was a metallic galumphing on the bleachers. Kasey and Stacey, followed by their best friend, Faith Benson, hurried toward them. The three nine-year-olds were a study in contrasts. Faith was blue-eyed and fair skinned with a cap of dark, curly hair. The twins were tan, blond and brown-eyed. They took after their mother, and were identical. But they'd confided to Jensen how to tell which was which. Stacey had an almost invisible scar at the edge of her hairline caused by a run-in with the corner of a table when she was a toddler. *S* for Stacey and scar. With bangs over it, no one could see, or tell her from her sister.

"Hi, Jensen," they said in unison.

"Hi," she answered, folding her arms across her chest.

"Hi, Daddy," the two girls said together.

"Hey, you two." He pulled them close, one on each side of him. "Hi, Faith."

"Daddy, we have a completely brilliant idea."

"Beyond brilliant," Kasey added.

"Is that right?" He sat down on the bleacher bench and settled the girls, one on each knee. Their friend stood watching.

"Dad, you're squishing me," Stacey complained.

"Me, too," said her sister, squirming.

"Sorry." The sheriff loosened his grip slightly.

Jensen studied him with his children. Was it just her imagination, or was he hanging on to them for dear life? As the girls chattered, she noticed that he scanned the crowd like a secret service agent protecting the president of the United States. This behavior was a complete contrast to the laid-back lawman he'd been a few minutes before receiving the papers.

If she was a betting woman, she'd wager that summons had something to do with his children.

"So that's why we think it would be a good idea for us to spend the night at Faith's house," Kasey finished.

"What?" he asked, turning his attention to the eager little girls.

"Weren't you listening, Dad?" Stacey brushed her hair off her forehead. "We want to spend the night at Faith's house."

"No," he said sharply. "I want you home."

Identical faces creased with disappointment. "But why?" they said together.

"My mom said it was okay," Faith added.

Jensen studied the girl and somehow knew that the little schemer was fibbing. She couldn't be sure whether or not it was a conspiracy.

"That's right," Kasey said. "We asked Maggie and she said it was okay with her if it was okay with you."

"She did, Dad," Stacey piped up. "Honest."

Aha, Jensen thought. Collusion. With malice afore-thought, if the knowing glances exchanged by the three amigos were anything to go by. He was being tag-teamed big-time. She recognized the technique because she and Taylor had done the same thing to their father until tutoring from their mom had wised him up. Did Grady have a clue what they were doing?

"I'll just go talk to Maggie and see what she has to say."

A superhero, able to leap conniving kids in a single bound. That was refreshing. Or maybe dealing with crackpots and criminals gave him the edge of cynicism he needed to keep their feminine wiles-in-training from overpowering him.

"Kasey, Stacey," Faith said, "I'll see you guys in a little while. I hafta go check in with my mom." Before Grady could stop her, she turned and raced down the stairs.

The twins started to wiggle off his lap, but he held on.

"Not so fast." He checked the arena, then looked at Jensen. "The final events are about to start. I have to go make sure that my staff is in place. It's been nice talking to you. I'll take the girls with me."

"Aw, Dad. We can take care of ourselves. It's so dumb hanging out with you when you're working. We'll die of boredom."

Which twin was it? Jensen wasn't sure. The speaker brushed her hair off her forehead and she identified Kasey.

Grady looked at the girl and tucked a strand of blond hair behind her ear. "Kase, I don't want you unsupervised. There are a lot of strangers here."

"So." The girl looked around. "We talked to a nice man just a little while ago. Remember, Jensen?"

"What man?" Grady asked sharply.

Jensen shrugged, trying to recall. "I was sitting here with the girls feeding them junk and braiding their hair and a man walked up to us."

"What did he say?"

"Small talk," she said. "He wanted to know if the girls were mine. He asked about you, where you were."

"What did you tell him?" he asked, frowning.

"That you're Destiny's sheriff."

"Anything else?"

Jen shook her head, but she'd been around the legal system long enough to know when she was being officially questioned. "You joined us right after that and he disappeared. I haven't seen him since."

"I want you guys to stay with me," he told the girls.

"Aw, Dad…"

"There's too many wackos and weirdos around," he said sternly.

"Dad, this is Destiny. Nothing bad happens here," Kasey said.

A muscle in his jaw contracted, but when he spoke, his tone was calm. "Mostly that's true. But sometimes stuff happens even here." He looked at each of his daughters in turn.

"We could hang out with Faith and Maggie," Stacey suggested.

Grady shook his head. "Maggie's busy with her booth. If she doesn't have customers, she'll be packing up. I can't take a chance."

Interesting choice of words, Jensen thought, noticing that the worry creases in his forehead deepened. What was going on?

Identical pairs of brown eyes focused on her. "Can we stay with Jensen?"

"I can't ask her—"

"Of course I'll keep an eye on them," she volunteered.

"Awesome," the two girls said together.

"Wait a second. I didn't give the all clear," he reminded them.

"But you're gonna. Right, Dad?"

He met Jensen's gaze. "You don't have to do this. I don't think boredom killed anyone yet."

When he looked like that, she wondered how she could say no to anything he asked. It bothered her until she remembered he hadn't asked. The girls had. But when she saw those two sweet, eager little faces, she couldn't say no to them, either. Like father, like daughter. She couldn't resist him—them. She meant them. He wasn't irresistible. She wouldn't let him be.

"I'd like spending time with the girls."

He smiled, and the tension in his face eased a bit. "Okay. I'm going to take you at your word. If you're sure—"

"I am."

"No more junk," he warned.

She put her hand over her heart. "I swear."

He kissed both of the girls, then left.

"Jensen, my French braid came out."

"Can you do my hair that way, too?"

"I would be happy to," she agreed. "I am woman—I can multi-task. But two at once would take more than my two bare hands. So one at a time. Okay?"

"Okay," they said together, giggling.

As she worked on twisting Stacey's hair into the intricate style, Jen scanned the arena. The final events had started. She wasn't sure who should be more grateful to whom. Grady to her for watching the girls while he worked. Or her to him for giving her a distraction against the onslaught of awful memories brought on by the imminent bull-riding competition.

And then there was the question of what was in that lawsuit that Grady O'Connor wouldn't talk to her about.

After the medical transport chopper left and he dispersed the milling crowd in the arena, Grady hurried into the stands to find his girls and Jensen. Ronnie Slyder was semiconscious after a run-in with the bull he'd ridden to win the competition. The teenager had been airlifted to a hospital twenty miles away. Hannah Morgan, the doctor who was filling in for Doc Holloway at the rodeo and in his office, had gone to the facility with Dev Hart to make sure everything medically possible was done for the kid. As Grady surveyed the area, he noted that the crowd had all but cleared out.

He wasn't sure whether or not that reassured him. Some creep was suing him, then he'd found out that a stranger had approached his girls and was asking questions. He didn't like this one bit. All he wanted was to get the girls home.

That was all he wanted until he took one look at Jensen's tense white face. No matter what he thought of the guy she'd married, Jensen had loved him and he'd been killed in an accident similar to the one tonight. Even though it was ten years ago, she would have to be a robot not to be shook.

He pulled the hand radio from his belt and pushed the button. "Deputy Haines?"

"Yeah, Sheriff?" a voice asked through his receiver.

"Meet me in the bleachers."

"Right." There was a click and the line was silent.

Grady walked up the stairs and greeted the girls. "Hey, you guys. Doin' okay?"

Two identical pairs of solemn brown eyes and one-of-a-kind serious green ones regarded him.

"Is Ronnie going to be okay, Daddy?" Kasey asked.

"I sure hope so, honey. I'm going to check on him as soon as I make arrangements to get you two home."

They both nodded and he was relieved that he wasn't going to get an argument. He'd had about all he could deal with tonight.

Deputy Haines walked up the several steps and joined them. He was young, just twenty-one, with black hair and blue eyes and a face that barely needed a razor. But he was trustworthy and would put himself between the girls and trouble. Grady would stake his life on it.

"What's up, Sheriff?"

"I want you to take my girls home and stay with them until I get there." He looked at them and noted the big yawns that meant there wouldn't be any arguments about bedtime. "Kasey, Stacey, I want you guys in bed, and don't give Deputy Haines any trouble. Got it?"

"Yes, sir," they said, their voices sleepy.

"I'll take good care of them, Sheriff."

"I know."

Grady watched the three as they walked down the stairs. At the far end of the arena a black-and-white SUV belonging to the sheriff's department was parked, and the three got in and drove away.

With a sigh, he sat next to Jensen. She still hadn't said a word. "You okay?" he asked.

"Fine." She reached up to tuck a strand of hair behind her ear. Her hand shook, putting the lie to the single word.

"Really?"

"Of course," she said, clamping her teeth together when she started to shiver.

Since the night was far from cold, he knew she was beginning to react. It was as if she'd held it together for the kids. Now that she was no longer responsible for them, she was letting go. Her whole body was trembling. He was really concerned about her.

Grady put his arm around her, pulling her against him. "It must have been awful when Zach died."

"Yeah. Awful."

"Tell me."

"N-no."

Grady had a strange sort of déjà vu feeling. The past was knocking up against the present. He wasn't sure why, but he was creeped out. First Mitch had come back and made things right with Taylor. Now Jen was here. The summons to answer a lawsuit that he'd received tonight. The bull-riding accident had obviously reminded her of losing the man she'd loved—and still did, if the look on her face was anything to go by.

That bothered him, and right now he was in no shape to analyze why. But one thing he knew—as much as he didn't want to hear anything in hushed, reverent tones about the jerk she'd married, he couldn't just walk away from her.

"Tell me what you're thinking," he urged, tightening his arm around her.

She looked at him with huge, haunted eyes. For a moment he thought she was going to refuse. Then she nestled against him and sighed.

"It was in Las Vegas. I hadn't seen him all day. We were supposed to meet before the rodeo, but..."

"What?" he prompted.

She hesitated and he waited for her to tell him that the creep had stood her up. That she'd seen him with another woman. That he'd made some lame excuse to avoid his responsibilities. All typical things he'd done when Grady had known him.

Then Jensen shrugged. "It's not important. I was in the stands. Like tonight. He had a good ride. The next thing I knew, he was on the ground as still as a stone."

A shiver shook her and he drew her into his arms, holding her against him, willing his warmth into her. He waited for her to speak again.

"I raced from the stands to the arena, but when I got there, he was already gone. They told me later he died instantly." She leaned back slightly and he loosened his hold. "It all came back tonight when I saw that boy lying there. Is he going to be all right, Grady?"

"Hannah said—"

"Hannah?"

"Dr. Morgan. She said his vital signs were strong but without diagnostic equipment that was all she knew."

"At least he was still alive. But…" Her expression was stricken.

"How about if I walk you up to the house and we'll call the hospital. See if they can give us any information on his condition."

"Okay." She started to stand, then hesitated. "You don't need to baby-sit me, Grady. I appreciate the shoulder to lean on, but I'm fine now. The twins need you, and I'm sure you're anxious to get home to them."

"Yeah. And I will." He stood up. "After I see you home and check on Ronnie."

"But…"

"I trust Deputy Haines. The girls are in good hands. They need to get some rest. In the morning we'll have a talk about it. I'll probably have some good news by then on Ronnie's condition." He held out a hand to her.

"You're not going to take no for an answer, are you?"

"Nope."

She put her hand in his and he pulled her to her feet.

A short time later they were standing on the front porch of the ranch house. When they'd arrived, Grady had found Mitch on the phone to the hospital. Ronnie was undergoing tests, but he was conscious and all the signs were good. Hannah had told him that tests were done as much to rule out problems as find them. She was optimistic that the teenager would be just fine.

Finally Jensen had insisted he go home to his girls and had walked him outside. The front porch was lit up like the town square at Christmas. He could see the shadows lingering in her eyes.

"Thanks for walking me home, Grady. I appreciate it. Tell the girls hello and give them a kiss for me."

He stared into her beautiful face for a moment, then before he thought it through, he leaned close and lowered his mouth to hers. First he tasted surprise on her lips and slid his arm around her waist to draw her closer. Fully expecting her to pull away, he wondered why she didn't. Then he stopped thinking at all and gave himself up to exploring the perfection of her mouth.

Lips as full and soft as clouds met his own. He tunneled his fingers into her hair, gently urging her to make the contact more firm.

She smelled so good. Her hair was like silken strands tangled in his fingers. The sound of her rapid breathing heated his blood as it raced through his veins. Her soft femininity lured him into a sensuous haze and he never wanted it to clear. Suddenly the front door opened, spilling more light onto the porch.

"Oops," Taylor said. "Sorry, Grady. I'll catch you later, Jen."

But Jensen instantly backed out of his arms. Then the light disappeared and a soft snick told him they were alone again.

Jen ran a shaky hand through her hair. "Why did you do that?"

The words, wrapped in her breathless, sexy voice, burrowed inside him, and all his nerve endings went on tactical alert. If he'd known the answer to her question, he would have answered it. But he didn't have a clue why he'd kissed her. More important, he didn't want to examine his motivation too deeply.

"I just wanted to take your mind off what happened

tonight," he said lightly. "Give you something else to think about."

"Replace a bad memory with a good one?"

"Is it a good one?"

"You're fishing for compliments again, Sheriff."

There was a trace of teasing in her tone, but it was forced. He could tell. In spite of the fact that she'd been married, there was an air of innocence about her. Hell of a quality for an attorney. But *innocent* best described her as far as he was concerned.

"Nope. Not me. Just trying to do a good deed."

"You're quite a combination of knight in shining armor and the guy in the white hat, aren't you?"

"It's a gift."

"Well, let me return the favor."

"Yeah? How?"

"That summons has something to do with the twins. Let me take a look at it so I can help."

Chapter Three

After making the statement, Jensen put some distance between herself and the sexy sheriff. She leaned her back against the front porch support and folded her arms over her chest, letting the evening breeze cool her hot cheeks.

Why had he kissed her? She didn't completely buy his selfless, good-guy act. On the other hand, she would rather believe he was chivalrous as opposed to attracted. Because she was infatuated enough for both of them, and that was so not what she wanted. If she let it, their meeting of mouths could be a life-altering experience and she had no reason to want her life altered in any way, shape or form.

He'd told her earlier his bachelor status was based on attraction and approval. He needed to be attracted to a woman that his girls approved of. So far that hadn't happened for him. Tonight she'd gotten along pretty well with the persnickety O'Connor twins— meaning one hurdle crossed. After that kiss, she issued an all-points bulletin to her heart—do not under any circumstances approach the suspect with the intention of apprehending his heart.

With that directive uppermost in her mind, bantering with him after that earth-moved-under-her-feet experience was the hardest thing she'd ever done. Her first legal argument in front of the toughest judge in Dallas had been a walk in the park by comparison.

Bringing up the summons he'd received earlier was the only thing she could think of to take the heat off herself and put it squarely back on him where it belonged.

She let out a long breath. "So what do you say, Grady? Want to talk about who's suing you and why?"

"No."

"Just like that? No? I thought you law-enforcement types were trained in methods of negotiation."

"You're thinking of the FBI."

"But don't they teach you how to interrogate perps, how to meet them halfway to get the information you want?"

He shrugged, and the shoulder movement did things to his body that made her knees weak. "It's not worth wasting your time."

"As an officer of the law you should know better. Anyone can bring suit. It's up to a judge to decide whether or not it has merit. That's where I come in."

She watched him rest a hip against the porch railing beside her, one booted foot grounding him, the other dangling back and forth. Very masculine. She made a conscious effort to inhale deep, calming breaths. If he was a couple of inches closer, she would be able to feel the heat from his body. The thought made her shiver, and she stepped up those deep, calming breaths.

After clearing her throat she said, "It's my job to convince the judge that whoever is suing you has no merit to his case."

"I can handle it."

"The worst thing you can do is be casual about this, Grady. It's about your children."

In the moonlight she saw him frown and the lines of his face tighten. "I never take anything about my children for granted. And don't look now, Counselor, but I haven't confirmed your guess that it has anything to do with them."

"It's more than a guess."

"How can it be?"

"The fact that right after getting those papers you were holding on to the girls so tightly they could hardly breathe. Then you sent them home with an armed guard. It couldn't have been more clear if you'd taken out a billboard on Interstate twenty." The worry lines between his eyebrows deepened. "You went from teasing to terrified in four little words—*You've just been served.*"

"Okay. You win."

"Yes, I do. More often than not. Every time I go into court I'm prepared. I've done my homework and try to make sure there are no surprises. I'm very good. So what gives, Grady?"

"Someone is suing me for custody of the girls."

The grim look on his face told her he was serious. Even though she'd had a feeling it was something like this, his confirmation of her suspicions surprised her. Only a relative would have a prayer of obtaining custody. Grady didn't have anyone else.

"Who would do something like this? Lacey's folks?" she asked.

"Her parents are both dead. There isn't anyone else. If that's what you're thinking."

"Actually I was thinking there's a name on those papers you received, and sharing it would be a big help."

"Not important," he said.

"Okay. If you won't tell me who, at least explain why."

"How should I know?"

She straightened away from the porch support and jammed her fists on her hips. "For a smart man, you're acting like a moron."

"Don't sweet-talk me, Jensen. Tell me how you really feel."

"You're an idiot."

"That was sort of a rhetorical comment," he said wryly. "I didn't realize you'd stoop to calling me names."

"If the shoulder holster fits…" She finished her statement with a shrug. "Look, Grady, I'm trained for this and I want to help. We're friends. Why won't you let me?"

"You don't have to take on the world's problems."

"I'm not. Just yours—"

"Where were we?" he interrupted. "Oh, yes. I was trying to replace a bad memory with a good one until your sister so rudely interrupted us." He put both boots on the wooden porch and took a step toward her.

She backed away and made a cross with her index fingers to ward him off. "A blatant attempt to side-track me and it's not going to work."

He grinned. "How will you know unless we try?"

If he continued to smile at her like that she would try anything and probably forget her own name. "Knock it off, Grady. This is serious. And you're not as charming as you think."

"Yes, I am."

Yes, he was. But it didn't quite distract her enough. She found it odd and disturbing that he wouldn't tell her anything about the lawsuit. Granted, they hadn't been close friends for years. But he'd seen how shaken she was when the teenage bull rider had been injured, and had stayed with her. A trusted deputy had taken his girls home. Even with the problem that had been dropped on him just that night, he'd flatly refused to leave her.

Her heart skipped at the thought and warmth spread through her that had nothing to do with a June evening in Texas and everything to do with how sweet and thoughtful Grady O'Connor was. After all these years on her own, his warm, supportive presence was like a light at the end of a long black tunnel. She just hoped the beam wasn't attached to a speeding locomotive.

"I'll take your silence as agreement on my charm," he said.

"I'm immune to charming men."

"Oh? Let's test that defense."

He put his arm around her waist and loosely settled her against his chest. Cupping her cheek in his big, warm hand, he started to lower his mouth to hers.

"I'm fine. I don't need the distraction." Jensen stepped away from the circle of his arms. "And you can't afford to take this situation lightly."

"It's just a nuisance suit." He shoved his hands into the pockets of his khaki pants.

"Probably. But if you don't take it seriously now, it could become more than that. Let me help. I can put together a strategy to convince the judge that the case is without merit and get it thrown out before it snowballs into something big. It's my job, and I'm very good."

"I'm sure you are. But you're good at it in Dallas, and I live in Destiny. I intend to seek legal counsel, but I'll get someone local to handle it. Besides, you're here on vacation."

"Not so fast, Sheriff. You know what they say about assuming something."

"What's that?"

"It makes an ass out of u and me."

He laughed. "In my case it's probably no more than the truth. But it would be less than gentlemanly to agree with that—about you."

"I'm not just here for a vacation. My firm is considering opening a branch office in Destiny."

"Is that so?"

"Yes, that's so. Business in the area is expanding outward from the Metroplex. Growth brings jobs, people, housing. Because I know the area, the firm sent me here to handle it."

"So your offer to help is testing the waters of legal expansion?"

"Of course not. I genuinely want to do what I can to advise you—legally. I've seen you with the girls. You're terrific."

"Thank you, ma'am."

"I didn't say that to flatter you. It's just the truth. I can't conceive of a good reason for anyone to initiate a suit like this. Tonight I saw for myself the love, discipline and just plain common sense of your parenting skills. We've already established it's not a relative of yours or Lacey's who's behind this. It would be a crime to take them away from you. No one could love them the way their biological father could.''

She saw the frown return to his face and missed the teasing look and the warmth it generated. What had she said? She'd sincerely meant the compliment.

"I'm grateful for the vote of confidence.''

"Look, even if I wasn't heading up the law office here I could handle this long distance. I can—''

"Look, Jen, don't think I don't appreciate the offer. And from one of the finest Dallas attorneys, too. But you're not the right lawyer for this case.''

This case? It was right up her alley—her specialty, so to speak. In the past few hours since he'd invaded her personal space, she'd seen firsthand his protective streak. First with the twins, then with her. Was he refusing her offer because he was trying to protect her? From what? What could anything about his twins have to do with her?

"Why am I not right?''

"Look, I've got to get home to the girls. Are you okay now?''

"I'm fine.'' Thanks to him.

"Good.'' He walked to the steps and glanced over his shoulder. "See you around.''

"Okay,'' she answered, bewildered. "'Night.''

The echo of his footsteps faded. Unfortunately her bad feeling didn't. If she were smart, she'd let this go. She should be grateful he'd pushed her away—saved her from herself, so to speak. He didn't want her help. She didn't want to be attracted to him. Even-Steven.

Now she could get back to life as she knew it—on

her own. But why after spending time with the sheriff did that seem so lonely?

The next day Grady walked in the front door of the sheriff's office, and Deputy Phoebe Johnson looked up.

"Hey, boss." Behind the counter, she leaned forward and rested her forearms on it.

"Hey. Everything quiet?" he asked her.

She nodded. "How was lunch?"

"I ran into an old friend. Jack Riley."

"I heard about him. Good-looking military type. He went into This 'n That and didn't come up for air till lunch. Something going on with him and Maggie?"

Maggie Benson was the owner of Destiny's gift shop.

"Hard to say," he answered.

"Why? You had lunch with them."

"So?" Grady stood in front of the counter separating the waiting area from the two buddy desks behind it. Computer equipment and paperwork littered the tops of the work spaces.

"So, put your legendary detective skills to work and tell me your observations."

The pretty, young, auburn-haired deputy met his gaze with a speculative one of her own. Her eyes were the color of Texas bluebonnets—somewhere between blue and lavender. She filled out the uniform better than any deputy he had. But wild horses would never get him to say that out loud. He treated her just like everyone else and that's just the way she wanted it.

At twenty-three, Phoebe was dedicated, smart and ambitious. Grady figured she was after his job. She'd probably have it someday, but not until he was ready to give it up. He was acting sheriff while elected sheriff Warren Drummond was on medical leave after a heart attack. But he would probably retire early, since his health was unlikely to permit him to return to the demanding job.

"My observations are that Maggie and Jack are friends."

Phoebe shook her head and slid him a pitying look. "If that isn't just like a man."

"You want to elaborate on that?"

"No."

He raised an eyebrow. "Let me rephrase. What does that mean, Deputy?"

"It means you wouldn't know a romance in progress if it sashayed up and hit you in the head with a two-by-four."

He grinned. She had a way with words and didn't mince any of them. Not unlike a sassy brunette he couldn't seem to get out of his mind. Thoughts of Jensen had kept him awake tossing and turning.

"I seriously doubt that there's anything going on between Jack and Maggie. Like I said, friends."

"That's not what Ginger Applewhite said."

Ginger clerked at Charlie's Tractor Supply for her owner husband. "What did she say and how did she know?"

Phoebe sighed. "She told me Jack O'Hunk stuck like gum on a boot heel to Maggie at the high school championships last night. Then today he shows up in town and disappears inside her shop. When they come out, he's not carrying a bag, which means he didn't purchase anything. So it was personal. Then they wind up having lunch together. What would you call *that*?"

"Circumstantial evidence."

"Not to me. It's love, plain and simple."

"There's nothing plain and simple about love."

Jensen was walking, talking, curvaceous, sexy proof of that statement. He didn't believe in love, but she'd spent a lot of years pining for a guy who wasn't worth the powder it would take to blow him to hell. What was plain and simple about that? Or the fact that Grady couldn't seem to get her out of his mind.

He might have been able to—at least, he'd have had a fighting chance if he hadn't been dumb enough to kiss her. What was that all about? And could he take it back?

But there was something about the way she'd looked standing on the porch in the moonlight. Something about the vulnerability peeking through the tough outer shell around her when she'd told him about the night Zach died. Something sad and brave that had tugged at him and made him want to fix what ailed her. Even though she'd tried to shrug it off, he knew the bull-riding accident had shaken her up.

He knew it as surely as he knew staying far away from her should be his modus operandi. Hard to do, considering her determination to help. He wished she would just leave it alone.

Phoebe tipped her head to the side as she studied him. "Is that experience talking? Macho baloney? Or are you just a confirmed bachelor?"

"The latter."

She nodded. "Yeah. Me, too."

"You? By gender definition you can't be a bachelor. Besides, I thought your motto was So Many Guys, So Little Time."

She smiled, a dazzling display of full lips and straight white teeth. "You heard that, huh? It's not that so much as my life is steady and on course. I don't need a—how can I put this? A nasty speed bump.''

''Me, either.''

Her gaze swung past his shoulder as she looked out the big window on downtown Destiny's main street. ''Don't look now, but here comes one. A speed bump, I mean.''

Grady half turned and heard a car horn honk as he spotted Jensen hesitate while she waited to see if the truck would stop for her. When it did, she hurried across the street. There was no hesitation as she opened the door to his office and came in. Her green eyes held anger, betrayal and confusion.

He straightened and went to her. ''What's wrong, Jen?''

''I need to talk to you.''

He took her arm and studied her. She was wearing a short-sleeved, light blue denim shirt tucked into jeans. He'd seen her legs in last night's sundress and somehow covering them seemed even more sexy, hiding her curves yet outlining them at the same time. After the way he'd left her last night, he hadn't expected she would voluntarily seek him out. His gut tightened and a knot of apprehension pressed on his chest.

''Are you okay?'' he asked.

She shook her head. ''I'm so not okay.'' She looked at Phoebe.

''Jensen Stevens, this is one of my deputies, Phoebe Johnson.''

The redhead nodded. ''Nice to meet you.''

Jen's polite smile was strained. ''Same here.'' She

looked up at him. "Is there somewhere private we could have this conversation?"

He put his hand at the small of her back. "Let's go in my office. Hold my calls unless someone's bleeding or on fire," he said to his deputy.

"You got it, boss."

He guided Jen down the hall and felt her trembling. What in the world was wrong? They passed three offices. When they reached the fourth, he turned her inside and closed the door behind them. His gray metal desk was littered with files and scattered papers. The computer monitor was on, displaying data from an unsuccessful search he'd initiated just that morning into the background of Billy Bob Adams. Unfortunately he'd turned up nothing of any use, which was why he'd asked for Jack Riley's help earlier at lunch. His old friend had been in the army—Special Forces. And a computer expert. Grady figured he could go places a small-town sheriff like himself couldn't. Especially with equipment from the Stone Age—relatively speaking.

"Sit down, Jen," he suggested, indicating one of the chairs in front of his desk. The metal frames with plastic-covered seats and backs didn't invite visitors to stay long. But it was all he could offer.

"I don't want to sit."

"Suit yourself." He took off his hat and placed it on the paperwork strewn across his desk. Then he rested a hip on the corner and folded his arms over his chest. "What can I do for you?"

Her eyes darkened to a shade of hunter green. "You can tell me what my dead husband's brother has to do with you and your children."

He felt as if he'd been sucker punched. "What are you talking about?"

"I hope nothing more than Destiny gossip."

"You're going to have to be a shade more specific."

"Someone overheard you talking to Jack Riley at the Road Kill Café a little while ago."

"Small-town communication system strikes again," he said grimly. "What about it?"

"The rumor is that Billy Bob Adams is the one suing you for custody of the girls."

He would feel less cornered if he'd been pinned down by the Hole in the Wall gang. A million things came to mind that he would rather do than have this conversation. With a little two-stepping and a bucket of grease maybe he could slide out of it. "And?"

"Is it true?"

"It's hearsay, Jen. Not permitted in a court of law."

"Don't patronize me, Grady. I know what hearsay is. I also know something felt weird from the time you got those papers."

"I've never been sued before. Of course I acted weird."

She wasn't going to let it drop. She was going to force him to tell her something that would rock her world. It was like drop-kicking a kitten, and he was going to hate himself forever for doing it to her.

"Don't you *dare* put your cop face on." She glared at him and tension starched every line and curve of her body. "Billy Bob is Zach's brother. Only a blood relative would have a chance of success in a case like this or no lawyer worth his salt would waste time with it. I need the truth, Grady. I need to know what's going on."

He let out a long breath. "Okay. You want it straight?"

"That's what I just said. Why would my dead husband's brother sue for custody of your children?"

"Because he's their uncle, Jen. Zach is the twins' biological father."

Chapter Four

Jen felt as if a tornado had dropped out of the sky and caught her up in the funnel of its spinning power and destruction. A fissure opened up in the foundation of the life she'd created. She wanted to collapse in the chair he'd offered her a few moments ago, but she'd trained herself not to show weakness.

"I was his wife," she said, her voice hardly more than a whisper no matter how much steel she tried to put in it. "I never heard anything of the kind. How could you say that?"

Grady ran a hand through his hair. "You don't need to hear all the ugly details."

"Yes, I do," she snapped. "I need to know the truth. It's been ten years and it's about damn time, don't you think?"

"What's the point? He's gone."

"The point is he was my husband." She rested a hand on the back of the chair and gripped so hard her fingers hurt. "I have to know what happened."

He let out a long breath and looked at the ceiling as if for divine intervention. Time seemed to stand still. Finally he nodded. "Okay. You win. It was during the high school rodeo championships, the last time we were all together—you, me, Jack, Mitch, Dev, your little sister. One night a bunch of us went to the lake to party."

She thought back to that year—the last time they'd all been together. Just before she'd run off and married Zach. Shaking her head, she said, "I don't remember."

"You weren't there. It was me, Jack Riley, Dev Hart. Mitch had just gotten the old one-two from the Stevens sisters. You dumped him, then Taylor pushed him in the pool. He was ready to get some of that out of his system, and he rounded us up to go to the lake. There were a few girls. Lacey was one of them. I tried to get her to stay home, but she wouldn't listen. Her dad wasn't there and it was her chance to have a little fun." He stopped. "Are you sure you want to hear this?"

It was as if Jensen had been transported back in time. She recalled that she and Zach had argued about her refusal to "put out," as he'd called it. He'd said he would find someone woman enough to give him what the all-around point winner was entitled to. Then he'd left.

Her heart pounded, palms grew slick and her legs turned to taffy. She steeled herself to show nothing.

"Go on," she said, pleased that her voice barely shook.

He studied her carefully, as if he could see into her soul and how much hearing and remembering that painful time was tearing her apart. It was like taking a stubborn Band-Aid off a deep cut—the slower you tugged, the more it hurt.

"Get it over with."

He nodded grimly. "We had a few beers. After competing in our events during the day, we let off steam at night. It was loud and crazy. Some of us wound up in the lake, splashing and hollering. Zach singled Lacey out."

It was coming, the biggest hit of all. She sealed her emotions away under a glass dome and numbed herself. It was the only way she could continue to probe.

"What about Zach—and Lacey?"

"She'd come with me, over my protest. But I promised myself I'd look after her. When the party broke up, we found Lacey huddled in the bushes. He'd refused to take no for an answer. They call it date rape today."

"No!"

He nodded. "We wanted to take him apart, but she wouldn't let us. Said it would raise too many questions. She'd die if her father found out. She made us promise not to do anything."

"But the twins? How can you know he..."

She couldn't finish the statement. Zach had fathered them? How could those sweet little girls be the result of something so ugly?

"She was a virgin, Jen. And after that night she was never with anyone else."

"How can you..."

"Know? I just do." He ground out the words. "The last night of the championships you eloped with Zach. No one knew where you were. Lacey was desperate when she found out she was pregnant."

"Oh, God…" She met his gaze. "Did Zach know?"

"Yes." He stood and looked down at her. "And I'm surprised."

"Join the club."

"That's not what I meant. You haven't come straight out and called me a low-down, rotten liar."

"I…" She swallowed hard. "How do you know for sure Zach did what you're saying? That he knew about the baby?"

"Besides the fact that Lacey wouldn't lie to me, he confirmed it. I saw him when he was back in town."

She nodded. "We made it home for a couple of days in between rodeos."

"I found Zach and his brother drinking beer one night behind Charlie's Tractor Supply. It's how Billy found out Lacey was pregnant and he was going to be an uncle."

"You fought with Zach, didn't you?" She remembered her husband had come home with a black eye, broken nose and split lip.

"Yeah."

"Tell me everything, Grady."

"Jen, there's no point—"

"I need to know!" She raised her voice, so unlike her. But this was unlike anything she'd ever been through. The illusion of the man she'd married, lost and kept in her heart for all these years was disintegrating. She wanted answers, and she wanted them now. "I have to know, Grady. Everything." Doubt and hesitation swirled in his blue eyes. "If you're my friend, you'll tell me the truth. All of it. Now. Please."

"Okay," he said, then let out a long breath. "He tried to tell me the baby wasn't his, that she'd slept with other guys. That's when I went after him.'' Tension turned his jaw to granite. ''She'd never been with anyone before. Zach forced her to do something she didn't want to do, then he tried to make her cheap.'' His voice was humming with anger, hard as nails.

She shivered, still unwilling to believe he was talking about Zach Adams. Her husband. The man she thought she'd known as well as she knew herself. This was a side to him she'd never seen. Or had she, and just ignored it?

Signs had begun to surface, a voice in the back of her mind said. Memories surged and twisted at the edge of her consciousness, but she didn't want to acknowledge them. She'd buried the feelings along with her husband. There'd been no good reason to deal with them. He'd died. But if he hadn't died, what then? What would have happened to their marriage?

Grady moved forward. Only the chair she still gripped stood between them. ''Jen, he gloated that he didn't have to take responsibility for the brat she was carrying because he was already married. He was proud of the fact he could duck any consequences.''

Guilt and pain twisted together in her gut. Had Zach urged her to run off with him because he'd *wanted* a shield from what he'd done? There was no way he could know a pregnancy would result. But still—

She looked up at Grady into blue eyes so cold she shivered. ''He could have been held responsible for child support.''

He shook his head. ''Lacey didn't want that, or anything to do with him. She was afraid no one would believe her. She was scared of the gossip, the way everyone in town would look at her. She wasn't strong like you. Delicate in body and spirit, like her name. Lacey."

The soft look on his face almost made Jen jealous. What would it be like to be loved the way he'd loved her? she wondered.

"She didn't want anyone, especially her father, to know what had happened to her. But she couldn't hide the pregnancy. I found her running away after her dad found out she was going to have a baby."

"And you married her. Because you loved her."

"I married her," he agreed. "We didn't find out until just before the birth that she was having twins. Then after they were born, there were complications. Lacey had just enough time to reconcile with her dad and make us both promise to raise her daughters together before she died."

Such a tragedy, she thought. Would Lacey still be alive if there hadn't been so much trauma attached to the pregnancy? She'd felt badly for Grady, losing his wife. He loved her so much, he'd married her in spite of the fact that she carried another man's babies. Now he was raising them alone.

Jensen couldn't think about it right now. Pain would wait. It always did. Sooner or later she would have to deal with it. But not yet. She would sort through it all later. What she had to do now was focus on the children. His daughters—Kasey and Stacey. Whatever had happened in the past didn't matter. Grady raised them and loved them. He was their father. An uncle who hadn't shown his face in Destiny for as long as she could remember was trying to take them away. It was wrong.

"I don't recall much about Billy," she said. "I haven't seen him for over ten years."

"Don't be so sure. It's been so long maybe you didn't recognize him. I think he was the guy who made small talk with you and the girls at the rodeo last night. Toying with you. Devious little sleaze…" He stopped and let out a long breath.

She frowned, trying to picture the stranger. "I sure couldn't pick him out in a lineup. I was distracted by the girls." But she shivered; the whole scenario gave her the creeps. "Even ten years ago—I don't have a memory of him."

"He's about four years younger than Zach. In trouble a lot trying to grab his share of attention from the fair-haired boy. Zach was a tough act to follow—first place in bull riding at the championships and all-around point winner. Billy had to get creative, since he didn't have anything else going for him. Still, his folks were the kind who believed their kid could do no wrong." He shrugged.

"Zach didn't talk about him."

Or much of anything else, she thought. That slipped out from under the protective seal over her feelings. It started to crack. Memories buried for years startled her. She pushed them away.

"Why now?" she asked. "The girls are nine years old. Why would he bring a custody suit now?"

"Who knows."

"But I just don't understand. Zach's folks left Destiny after he died, and my sister let me know when they both passed away. I always assumed Billy had gone with them. What would make him surface here and now?"

"I have a hunch it has something to do with an article that was in the paper recently."

"What article?"

"About your sister's dude ranch. Dev and I were there when Taylor was interviewed for the piece. There was a photographer who snapped a picture of the three of us and they put in a few facts about our ranches, how successful they are. I think he saw the article. That triggered memories. And maybe he saw an opportunity."

Jensen's eyebrows rose. "You think it's about the ranch?"

"Of course. What other reason could there be? For nine years he's been a no-show. Then he comes across the article and sees a way to cash in."

"I don't get it. Why wouldn't he try to get you to pay him off? Keep it quiet. Protect the girls."

"He wants the whole enchilada—the ranch."

"That's it, then," she said. "He can get his hands on the land through the girls. And he's a blood relative."

Jensen had lost her illusions, but he was looking at losing his children. To a scheming creep. Who was related to the man she'd mourned for so long. Grady must think she was the world's biggest fool.

"Look, Jen," he said, moving around the chair. He curled his fingers around her upper arms and tried to pull her against him, but she held herself stiffly away from him. "I'm sorry. I never meant for you to know any of that."

The last thing she wanted or deserved was his pity. Surely he had nothing but contempt for her. "I have to go."

"Let me take you home. This has been a shock. You're in no condition…"

"No." She walked to the door.

"Okay. I understand why you feel that way about

me. I'll get one of my deputies to drive you. Phoebe can—"

"I'm fine," she said, not feeling fine at all.

She wanted to be alone as fast as she could arrange it. His offer to drive her home was no more than automatic courtesy. She had to be the last person he wanted to be around. Married to the man who'd hurt the woman he'd loved. All these years she'd been foolish enough to mourn a man who'd deserved a punishment so much more than the black eye and fat lip Grady had given him.

Grady must hate her. He was a good man, a man who'd raised twin girls he'd known weren't his as if they *were* his own. She'd never guessed they didn't belong to him. And she'd had the nerve to say that no one could love them the way their biological father could. How could he stand the sight of her?

"I have to go," she said again, and hurried out of the office.

It was almost dinnertime before Jen finally walked through the front door of the Circle S. After leaving Grady earlier that afternoon, she'd driven around for hours thinking about the past. Now she needed to talk to Taylor and Mitch.

She turned left toward a sitting area with a huge stone fireplace and overstuffed furniture. Just before she entered the room, the sound of giggling and a man's deep-throated chuckle warned her.

"Hello?" She called out, then hesitated, giving Taylor and Mitch time to straighten clothing and stop any intimate behavior not appropriate for public consumption.

"Are you two decent?" she asked, entering the room.

On the sofa, Taylor sat on Mitch's lap with his arms around her. He was nuzzling her neck and her blouse gapped open where several buttons were undone. So much for her warning.

Envy nipped at Jen. She couldn't stop it, even though her sister deserved every bit of happiness she could grab with both hands. As for herself, she didn't have a right to it. All the thinking she'd done since leaving Destiny that afternoon had convinced her of it.

She stopped in the doorway, waiting for the couple to notice her and cease cuddling. They didn't. She remembered Grady kissing her on the front porch and her sister's comment when she'd opened the front door.

Jen cleared her throat, loudly. "Oops."

Instead of jumping apart, Taylor looked up and grinned. "Hey."

"Hi, Jen," Mitch said, tightening his hold on the woman in his lap.

"Hi, you two."

They reminded her of Sandra Bullock and Matthew McConaughey. Or maybe it was the happiness lighting their faces that made them so beautiful. She was glad Taylor had finally found someone to love. Correction—she'd found him ten years ago and a decade later he'd finally gotten the message.

"We're making wedding plans," Taylor said.

Jen smiled, then turned up the wattage to erase the sadness she knew was around the edges of it. "Didn't look to me like there was a lot of talking going on."

"You'd be surprised," Mitch said, tucking a strand of hair behind his fiancée's ear.

Jen released a big sigh and sat down on the sofa at a right angle to the couple. "After today, I'm not sure anything would surprise me."

Taylor straightened out of Mitch's arms. "What's wrong? You look like you lost your only friend."

She didn't know about only, but Grady sure as shootin' wouldn't want anything to do with her. How could he? It didn't matter that he'd been nice to her just last night. She'd forced him to reveal the past—now both of them had to face it.

"I found out something today," she said hesitantly. She met Mitch's gaze. Grady had said he knew everything. But the facts had stayed secret all these years. She wasn't sure he would want anyone else to know. "Mitch, can I talk to you for a minute? Privately."

He glanced at the woman still in his arms. "I'd rather Taylor stayed. We made a pact to not keep secrets. If you can't tell both of us, then…"

"I'm sure this secret is going to come out anyway." Lawsuits were public record. "What do you know about Zach and Lacey Miller?"

The expression on his face confirmed without words what Grady had told her. "How did you find out?"

"I overheard some gossip in town and I made Grady tell me," she said.

"Tell you what?" Taylor asked. "What's going on?"

"Billy Bob Adams is suing Grady for custody of the twins," Jen told her.

"But that's ridiculous. What right does he have?" Taylor looked from her to Mitch.

He linked his fingers together and rested them on

her abdomen, holding her to him. "Zach was their father."

He recounted the facts without interruption, and Jen figured it was because her inquisitive sister was too shocked to say a word. "Dev, Jack and I kept quiet out of respect for Grady's wishes. That and the fact we all felt guilty," he finished.

"Why?" Jen wanted to know.

"There were screams that night. But none of us recognized a cry for help. We were throwing each other in the lake, hollering and yelling ourselves. Every last one of us felt we should have done something to help Lacey, to protect her from that son of a—"

"Mitch…" Taylor warned him against dumping on her sister's beloved dead husband.

"Don't worry, Tay. That's being kind."

"Did he hurt you?" Mitch's voice was one step up from a growl.

Jen wasn't sure what had clued him in to the fact that all hadn't been perfect between them. But what she'd learned today had shown her she'd been pretending all these years. She was tired of it.

"It wasn't a fairy tale," she admitted.

Taylor wiggled off his lap and sat down next to her, draping an arm across her shoulders. "Maybe it's time to get it off your chest," she suggested gently. "It's been ten years. That's long enough to protect the memory of a guy who obviously doesn't deserve it."

Jen looked into her sister's sympathetic brown eyes and found she wanted to talk about the things she'd kept inside for so long.

"Toward the end, I think I knew the marriage might have been a mistake," she began.

"Why didn't you say something?" Taylor gasped.

"I didn't want Mom and Dad to know I'd screwed up. I didn't want to disappoint them."

"But what about you?" Mitch asked.

She shrugged. "Dad always said suffering the consequences of your actions defined character. I'd made a doozy of a mistake, and suffering the consequences in silence seemed nobler than whining. Besides, a part of me loved him very much. Even though…"

"What?" Taylor prompted.

"I found evidence of the women. He flirted even when he knew I was there. I saw lipstick on his collar that wasn't my shade. More often than not he'd come in at night with liquor on his breath and unfamiliar perfume on his clothes. But he said it was nothing. He loved me."

"Damn him," Taylor said. "You should have left him."

Jen smiled sadly. "I probably would have. But then he died. I was young, and at the risk of being a walking, talking cliché—really stupid."

"You should have talked it over with me," Taylor scolded gently.

"What was the point?" Jen asked, shrugging.

"The point is we tell each other everything and you shouldn't have carried this around by yourself all these years," her sister said.

"He sure as hell wasn't worth it," Mitch agreed.

"And don't I feel like the world's biggest, dumbest fool," Jen finished. "It's no wonder Grady refused my help with the custody suit."

"At least tell me about that," Taylor said. "You owe me."

"Okay. We were sitting together in the stands when

he was served with the papers," Jen started. "I practically had to drag the information out of him. He tried to pretend it was no big deal. But I knew better, by the way he was acting. Even when he gave me the facts, he tried to gloss over it. But in the Road Kill Café he asked Jack Riley to use his computer expertise and equipment that wasn't five years out of date. Maybe call in a favor to check out Billy on the Internet. Grady already tried his sources through the sheriff's office and came up with zilch. He figured Jack had access to files he couldn't open."

"And you know this how?" Taylor asked.

"Bonnie Potts told me," Jen said. "I heard her talking to Charlie Applewhite and she was more than happy to share the information with me, too. Then I went to see Grady."

"And you offered legal counsel?" Mitch asked.

She nodded. "He said I wasn't the right lawyer for this case. Now I know why. He thinks I'm too gullible."

"I'm sure that's not true," Taylor said. "He's just protecting you. I think he's got a thing for you."

Jen jumped up and backed away. "Don't go there. I have no intention of getting involved with a man ever again. Even if Grady was willing, which he told me he's not, there's just too much baggage. On my part. Obviously my judgment leaves a lot to be desired. Bottom line—I don't ever want to fall in love again."

"Have you ever heard that saying about protesting too much," Mitch said with a wicked grin.

Jen shook her head. "The jerk I had the bad sense to marry took a lot from Grady. We'll never know, but it wouldn't surprise me if the stress of all that happened wasn't responsible for the postbirth complications that took Lacey from him.''

"You were as innocent as Lacey," Taylor said.

"But I *feel* responsible."

"Stupidity isn't a crime," Mitch pointed out dryly.

Jen laughed. She couldn't help it. "Thank you, Counselor, for putting that into perspective with the proper legal spin."

"Any time," he said, grinning.

Taylor smiled at him, a look brimming over with love. "I'm marrying the comic relief. It sort of makes you proud, doesn't it? This probably isn't the right time, but—Jen, will you be my maid of honor?"

"Of course," she said simply, sitting down and hugging her sister. "Speaking of timing, mine sure is lousy. The last thing I want to do is bring you guys down when you're so happy."

Mitch grinned. "We're so happy, I don't think you *could* bring us down."

For several moments they discussed plans for the wedding. Jen's mind drifted to Grady and what he must be going through right now. Her heart went out to him.

"Earth to Jen." Taylor met her gaze. "I know that look. What have you got up your sleeve? What are you going to do?"

"Actually the question is what am I *not* going to do. The answer is—I'm not going to walk quietly away. I can easily find out when the court date is going to be. No matter how Grady feels about it, he can't arrest me if I show up for the preliminary custody hearing."

Chapter Five

Grady walked into the courtroom with his lawyer. He'd been there countless times to testify in criminal procedures, but never for a personal reason. But he knew everything was going to be fine. Soon this would be history, a bad dream. This was Destiny. Where the philosophy was if it ain't broke, don't fix it. No court would take his kids away.

He glanced down at the gray-haired attorney by his side. Clark Livingston had been practicing law in Destiny for fifty years. Shouldn't that count for something? But he knew Billy Bob Adams had convinced a hotshot Dallas lawyer that he had a claim to the twins. Jen was a hotshot Dallas lawyer, too. Grady wondered if he *should* have taken her up on her offer of help.

It wasn't just the promise he'd made to Lacey. He loved those kids more than anything else in the world. If there was any chance at all he could lose them—

As he moved down the aisle between rows of

wooden benches, a subtle fragrance of flowers caught his attention. Something light, sexy—familiar. He followed the scent to his right and saw Jensen Stevens. Before he could put his "cop face" on, she could have seen the involuntary pleased expression in his eyes. He knew for a fact his pulse kicked up at the sight of her.

It had been two weeks since she'd charged into his office demanding the truth. Odd that he knew exactly how long; maybe because they'd talked about the past. Then again, maybe not so strange. He'd felt like slime for destroying her good memories of the man she loved. It wasn't a feeling he particularly liked and a man tended to remember things like that.

So why the heck would she be in court today? Surely she wasn't there to support Zach's brother? He shook his head. No way. But, damn it. He didn't want her involved in this. Zach Adams was gone, but Grady didn't want the bad he'd left behind to touch her. His attorney continued down the aisle and set his briefcase on the wide table facing the judge's bench. Grady hesitated a moment, then started to move past her.

Jen stood up and put her hand on his arm. "Hi."

He froze and looked at her slender fingers on the sleeve of his suit coat. He'd dressed like a man going courting. A corner of his mouth lifted at the pun. He *wished* a pretty lady had been responsible for the red power tie around his neck. But his Sunday-go-to-meetin' clothes were all he could think of to tip the scales in his favor. It was about keeping his girls, not showing Jen he could play in society big leagues. Besides, she was the last person he'd expected to see. Not that she wasn't a sight for sore eyes, a fact he pushed down before it could get a toehold inside him.

"Why are you here?" he asked.

"To help."

"I've got an attorney."

One corner of her full mouth rose as she glanced at the older man setting papers on the table. "Far be it from me to bad-mouth another member of my own profession. God knows the public at large does that to all of us in general."

"Then don't," he said, knowing what she was thinking. He'd gone there himself before concluding that he didn't have a whole lot of choice.

"Clark Livingston has to be seventy-five years old," she pointed out. "He's practiced law here in Destiny since the ink dried on his license half a century ago. I'm the first person to sing the praises of experience. But he does wills, property-line disputes, deed transfers and some minor misdemeanor criminal stuff. In a nutshell, his practice is general. You need someone who specializes in family law. Someone who knows it inside and out. You need me," she said emphatically.

"Why do you want to do this?"

"Because you're my friend," she said.

He stared into green eyes so serious and sincere and heart-wrenchingly beautiful that it hurt. Standing straight and tall and proud, she was the prettiest thing he'd ever seen. And he'd missed her. How was that for having his crosshairs not lined up? She'd barely breezed back into town and he'd seen her a couple of times. Why would he miss her? Or need her? Lord help him, the word *need*—her word—was too darn close to the truth. And he wasn't talking legal representation. He also wasn't giving in to the feeling. Because they were friends.

He rubbed a hand across the back of his neck, grazing his starched white collar. "I appreciate the offer. But it's really not necessary. I'm sure this hearing is just a formality. In a few minutes it will all be over."

"But what if it's not? This concerns me, too."

Was she worried about him trashing her dead husband's reputation? She'd seemed sympathetic to Grady's situation the last time he'd seen her. Even though he'd had to set her straight about her scum-sucking husband. Had she thought it over and changed her mind?

He removed her hand from his arm, holding it for just a moment before letting go. "No one is taking my girls."

"Grady, please—"

"I have to go." But he figured he should give her fair warning. In case there *was* a chance. "I'll take his whole family down if I have to. So now's the time to get out if…"

She shook her head slightly. "You're not planning to do something desperate, are you?"

"Do I look desperate?" he asked. Lying didn't come easy to him and he had a suspicion he looked just as bad as he felt. But not for the reason she thought.

"Yeah," she confirmed. "You look like a man who could do something rash and reckless."

"Define reckless."

She eyed him speculatively. "If you were facing criminal charges I'd call you a flight risk."

"Why would I run?" he asked. He'd do it, if that's the way the dust settled. If push came to shove, he was prepared to do whatever was necessary to keep his children with him—and safe. But he really didn't expect it to come to that.

"You'd take off, because you're one of the good guys," she answered. "Sounds like a contradiction, but I think you know what I mean."

He did. And was glad she thought so. It was also the reason he wanted her to leave. To keep her as far from the ugliness as he could. "I appreciate the vote of confidence. But I don't need it. This hearing won't amount to a hill of beans. The judge will dismiss the case. Possession is nine-tenths of the law."

"Custody cases are unpredictable and it doesn't matter who's got possession of the kids or for how long."

"Objection noted. But I really do have to go."

Before she could rebut, and before he didn't have what it took to walk away from her, he turned and joined his *experienced* attorney in the front of the room. Age and wisdom must count for something, he thought. Just like Jen said. He sat down beside his lawyer and faced the judge's bench. Why did it feel so much like being a teenager facing the music?

When the fiftyish, blond woman in a flowing black robe took her place on the bench, Grady sucked in a deep breath and braced himself. He knew her. She was caring and fair.

"All rise for the Honorable Judge Rebecca Kellerman," the bailiff's deep voice echoed.

She settled herself, then looked at the sparsely filled courtroom. "I'm ready to hear arguments from both sides," the judge announced.

Grady's lawyer was first and outlined all the reasons the suit should be thrown out. Grady O'Connor had raised the girls from birth. He was the only father they'd ever known. It was paramount to maintain stability for the children. And it had been the birth mother's dying wish for him to take her children.

Then it was the slick Dallas attorney's turn. He made a case that genetics should be taken into consideration. His client was their blood kin, and wasn't it better for children to be raised by a relative? Since Sheriff O'Connor wasn't kin, could it be he kept the children because it gave him access to the prosperous ranch on their mother's side?

Grady's lawyer countered that the twins had never met their uncle. How did anyone know for sure he *was* kin? Where had he been all this time? The lawsuit was frivolous and without merit. It was a waste of the court's time to even consider it.

Finally the judge held up her hands for quiet. "Gentlemen, the arguments on both sides are compelling. Children need stability and the only good reason for upsetting the applecart *is* family. The importance of roots can't be discounted—"

"Your Honor, may I confer with counsel?"

The soft, sexy female voice sent hot and cold running need up and down Grady's back. He turned and looked at Jen. What the hell was she up to?

The judge peered over the granny glasses on the end of her nose. "Who are you?"

"I'm an attorney. I was married to Zach Adams, the man who allegedly fathered the twins in question."

"You may approach."

Jensen walked forward, through the swinging wooden gates. She met Grady's gaze, then bent her head and whispered to his attorney, who nodded.

"What's going on?" he asked.

Clark held up his hand for quiet. Frustration gnawed

at Grady's gut. In about two seconds he could take his quiet and shove it.

Finally the judge cleared her throat. "I don't have all day, Counselor."

Jen slid Grady an unreadable look just before she walked back to the spectators' chairs and sat.

Clark stood. "Your Honor, we'd like to request that DNA testing be done on all parties involved to establish beyond any shadow of doubt paternity of the twins in question."

"But I thought the father was deceased," the judge said.

"That's true. But DNA is in every cell of the body—including hair. Miss Stevens has kept a lock of her husband's. That will provide a sample for examination. We submit that Sheriff O'Connor, the twins and Mr. Adams also be tested. Then we'll know exactly where we stand and can proceed accordingly."

Grady stood up, his nerves raw. "No one is contesting paternity." What did she hope to gain by providing the enemy with ammunition?

"Sit down, Sheriff. You should know I don't permit outbursts in my courtroom."

"Emotions are running high," Clark said. "It's true, no one has questioned the father's identity. But the claim has cast some doubt about the deceased's reputation. His widow would like to know the truth—whatever it might be."

Judge Kellerman leaned forward. "His widow isn't a petitioner in the case."

"Also true." Clark cleared his throat. "But isn't it in the best interests of the children for *all* the facts to be known?"

The judge was quiet for several moments. "Gentlemen, after taking everything into consideration, it's still my opinion that family *is* important and shouldn't be discounted.''

Grady couldn't breathe. This wasn't good. Certainly not what he'd expected.

Judge Kellerman looked from one table to the other. ''I'm ordering that DNA tests be done on the girls, the man who claims to be their uncle, Sheriff Grady O'Connor who now retains custody, and the deceased who is allegedly the father. When the results are in we will reconvene to hear them. We'll go from there. Thank you, gentlemen.''

She swept out of the courtroom and Grady didn't know whether to heave a sigh of relief or not. No one had ordered him to surrender the girls. But it wasn't over as easily as he'd expected, either.

He glanced over his shoulder. The courtroom was empty. Jen was gone. What in the world had she been thinking? She'd convinced him she was sympathetic to his situation and sincerely wanted to help. He just didn't understand how proving beyond a shadow of a doubt that Billy was their biological uncle would do him any good.

''What now?'' he asked his lawyer.

''Like the judge said—DNA tests,'' Clark answered. ''I'll arrange for that with Dr. Morgan.''

''How long will it take?'' Grady asked.

''Haven't a clue. Never done this before,'' he mumbled, scratching his snow-white head. ''Hard to keep up with modern science.''

Grady would have bet his sheriff's badge Jensen knew how long tests like that would take. Maybe he could... Nope, he wasn't going there. This wasn't her baby to rock. And he planned to tell her so.

"I need to talk to someone," Grady said.

"You do that, son. In the meantime, I'll do some research on case law for this. See if I can find a precedent in our favor. But I gotta tell you, I've never run across anything like this situation in all the time I've been practicing law."

Great. Just what he'd wanted to hear. How to win confidence and influence destiny, Grady thought ruefully. He'd expected the case would be thrown out and it hadn't been. Jen had said custody cases could be unpredictable. She was young, smart and this was what she did for a living. She'd offered to help him retain custody. Yet, she'd convinced the judge to order DNA tests. If he'd officially accepted her legal assistance, could she have hurt his cause more? Why would she do this to him? There was no rhyme or reason to it. Any more than there was justice in the fact that she stirred his blood as no woman ever had.

"I'll see you later, Clark."

The older man nodded absently as Grady turned away. Stepping outside, Grady waited several moments for his eyes to adjust to the bright light. He took his mirrored sunglasses from his suit pocket and put them on. That was when he spotted Jen talking to Billy Bob Adams. They were standing in the shade, by the stone wall of the courthouse dominating the square in the center of downtown Destiny.

A red haze swallowed Grady whole. He didn't want that low-life creep anywhere near Jen, let alone smiling his sleazy smile at her. Then Billy touched her hair, tucking a strand behind her ear. Grady saw her shudder and duck her head away. It was all the excuse he needed.

He was beside them in two strides, just in time to

hear the jerk say, "How about I buy you a beer? To say thanks for what you did in there."

Grady stepped in front of Jen. He insinuated himself between her and harm, then grabbed the front of Billy's shirt. "Get the hell away from her."

Fear chased the self-satisfied, predatory look from Billy's face. "Grady O'Connor, as I live and breathe," he said in a shaky voice.

"You have no idea how much I wish I could change that," Grady growled. "Get away from her."

Billy held up his hands in surrender. "Am I steppin' on toes? I had no idea she was your woman. Just trying to be friendly to a pretty lady."

Grady ignored the insinuation. "Like at the championships? When you were talking to *my* girls?"

"*My* nieces," he countered.

"What the hell are you up to, Adams?"

"They're my family."

"If you really cared about them, you'd have shown up years ago." Rage billowed through him. "You won't get away with this."

"That's for the court to decide."

Two small hands gripped his arm, squeezing. Through his all-consuming fury he became aware that someone shook him. He looked down into Jen's worried green gaze.

"You shouldn't talk to him outside of court, Grady. Back off."

"Yeah, do as the lady says."

"Shut up." Jen glared at him. "Don't you ever come near me again."

The man held out his hands in a pleading gesture. "But we're practically family. You're my sister—"

"No!"

Because she was still holding his arm, Grady felt her tremble. He let Billy go and put an arm around her shoulders, tucking her snugly against his side.

Grady pointed at the other man. ''If you know what's good for you, you'll drop this whole thing and get the hell out of Destiny. And never show your face around here again or I'll make you sorry you ever started this.''

''Is that a threat, Sheriff?''

''It's a promise, Adams.''

''We'll see about that.'' He shoved his fingers through his sandy hair as resentment flared in his shifty pale blue eyes. He was short, wiry and had weasel written all over him.

Grady could smell the type a mile away. Chip on his shoulder. Figured the world owed him a living. A coward who took the easy way out. And the blackest mark against him: he was related to the man who'd caused this whole stinking mess in the first place. The only good to come out of it was the twins.

Without another taunt or threat, Billy brushed the back of his hand across his mouth, then walked down the courthouse steps and got into a battered old truck parked in the lot. After starting the motor, he gunned the engine, then hit the gas and with a screech of tires left the lot.

Jen watched him with a look of distaste on her face. ''Good riddance to bad rubbish,'' she said.

Grady dropped his protective arm. ''You could have fooled me.''

She shielded her eyes from the sun as she looked up at him. ''What's that supposed to mean?''

''I just saved your bacon, Counselor. And after what

you did in that courtroom, I can't for the life of me figure out why.''

"I was doing just fine on my own, Sheriff.'' Her eyes glittered like emeralds. "And to set the record straight, I believe I saved *your* bacon in that courtroom. Or at least I threw it in the frying pan.''

"I'll go along with that. I just hope we're not out of it and into the fire on account of you.'' He loosened his tie. "Where in the world did you get the bright idea that DNA tests to *prove* that Billy is a blood relative would help?''

"Yeah, if—''

"If you didn't believe me about Zach, why didn't you just say so?''

"If I didn't believe you, I would have called you a liar to your face,'' she shot back.

Her eyes zinged daggers in his direction. She took his breath away—angry as all get-out, but so punch-to-the-gut beautiful it was all he could do not to pull her into his arms. How stupid was that?

"And you figure that stunt you pulled helped me—how?'' he asked, trying to find some distance from her.

"Don't you see, Grady? The family tie weighed pretty heavily with the judge.''

"Yeah, I noticed.''

"Your lawyer's argument was…''

"The judge said it was compelling,'' he pointed out.

"As far as it went.''

"So you rode to the rescue like the Lone Ranger.'' She grinned. "I like that.''

"It wasn't a compliment,'' he said. He knew what he was doing. It didn't take a hundred-dollar-an-hour shrink to tell him he was arguing with her on purpose to push her away. "Just what the hell did you think you'd accomplish by suggesting the damn DNA test, bright eyes? Or maybe I should call you Benedict Arnold?"

"I bought you some time, Sheriff."

"And just how do you think that's going to help? It won't change the facts. I've got Jack working on the case."

"Jack just found out he has a daughter."

Grady ran a hand through his hair. "I heard. He's the father of Maggie Benson's daughter."

"Yeah," she agreed. "That's a pretty major distraction and he'll need some time to deal with it. We need to cut him a little slack. But we can't stop trying to come up with something on Billy."

"Damn it," he said. "If I could convince the city council to increase my budget, I'd have computer technology that isn't—"

"Nearly as old as Clark Livingston?"

He ignored her. "By the time I can upgrade, maybe I'll be able to bring the department into the twenty-first century."

"More important than the equipment are Jack's contacts. He'll find something. If he's got the time to look."

Grady didn't like the worried expression marring the smooth skin of her forehead. After the unexpected turn of events in court, his confidence wavered. "You think the judge is going to give him custody?"

"I think he's got some explaining to do. Like where he's been for the last nine years. You said he was in trouble as a juvenile. Wouldn't surprise me if he's got a record."

"Because a leopard can't change his spots," he agreed.

Jen was on his side. Relief spread through him like warm on a sunny day.

She nodded. "There's no reason to believe he's an upstanding citizen now. You checked him out and couldn't find diddly. With Jack's contacts and expertise, he can go where a small-town sheriff has never gone before. I'm convinced he'll find something useful. If he's got some space."

He nodded. "Okay."

"Okay? That's all you can say? What about you think I'm brilliant? Then there's the ever-popular you don't know what you'd have done if I hadn't had the audacity to stick my nose in where it didn't belong in the courtroom? And how about—"

He tapped her nose. "It's awfully cute." Her mouth was open but no words came out. "What? Nothing to say, Counselor?"

He wished she would say something, because he so wanted to pull her against him. The memory of how good it felt to kiss her was never far from his mind. He wanted to do it again. Badly. He'd wanted to put his hands around Billy's neck and squeeze because he'd had the nerve to touch her. How was that for the town sheriff sworn to uphold the law?

Jensen Stevens did things to him, things he'd never experienced before.

She took a deep breath. "You showed a lot of restraint when you came storming out of the courthouse. I thought you were going to deck him—on account of the girls," she added.

He took his suit jacket off and slung it over his shoulder, holding it by one finger. With one hand occupied, it would be a bigger challenge to take her in his arms. "I wanted to deck him," he admitted. "I heard what he said when he touched your—touched you."

Her forehead wrinkled as she thought. Then she nodded. "The beer thing."

"Yeah."

"Is that what made you think I was on his side?"

"It didn't help."

"Don't you worry your pretty little head. I'd rather chew off my own arm than have a brewski with sludge like him." She shivered. "So you wanted to deck him on my account?"

"Yeah," he said, even though her smile said she was teasing. He couldn't stop himself. As soon as the single word was out of his mouth, he wanted it back in the worst way.

What had made him admit that out loud? To her? Confusion had dogged him ever since she'd come back to Destiny. He'd never experienced the gut-wrenching, knock-you-for-a-loop, want-to-be-with-someone-every-waking-moment kind of thing for a woman. He'd made peace with the fact that those feelings wouldn't happen to him.

Somehow, from the second she'd driven up in her sporty BMW, she'd sneaked inside him and snagged his attention before he knew what was happening. But Jensen Stevens, Destiny's golden girl, was the kind of woman he would spend his whole *life* not having. Prevention was the best treatment; he couldn't hope for a cure. No, his best bet was finding a way to resist her.

"Now that you know whose side I'm on, let me take this opportunity to tell you that I'll give you a professional discount for my legal services."

"Forget it, Jen." He took her elbow. "I'll see you safely home."

She pulled her arm away. "Number one, I'm not going home. Number two, why should I need you to see me anywhere? Number three, you want to tell me how I can forget it?"

"Billy is out there somewhere and I don't trust him as far as I could throw him. He messed with you and the girls once. I don't plan to let him get another chance."

"My hero."

He got the feeling she wasn't being a smart aleck, and the compliment warmed his blood and sent it racing through his veins, mostly to points south.

"So why should I forget about the case?" she asked.

He ran a hand through his hair. "We've already been over this. I don't—"

"Want you involved," she interrupted and finished for him.

"So if you already know, why did you ask?"

"Because you're a little late. I'm already involved."

"And whose fault is that?" He rolled up his right shirtsleeve, then switched his jacket to the other hand while he did the left. He sighed. "Look, Jen. I don't mean to sound ungrateful. Thanks for your help today. But I can take it from here."

He'd underestimated things today. But from here on in, he would channel all his efforts into the fight. The only upside would be that he wouldn't have any energy left over to think about a luscious brunette with eyes as green as a Texas prairie in springtime. Made no sense to waste time on something he could never have.

But he had to admit, he'd expected the custody question to be decided in his favor by now. He was beginning to wonder if refusing Jen's help wasn't the classic cut-off-his-nose-to-spite-his-face scenario.

She folded her arms over her breasts. "Are you going to see me where I *am* going?"

"And where is that?"

"Across the street to my new office."

"Okay. I can do that."

"Good. Because I plan to make a convincing argument to show you why you're one bullet short of a full clip."

Chapter Six

Jen walked down the courthouse steps with Grady beside her. When they got to the bottom, he moved around her so that he was closest to the street. The courtly gesture, so automatic to him, stirred a warm, gooey feeling in the pit of her stomach. And that wasn't all. Even though it was a spectacularly beautiful June day in Texas, she had absolutely no right to be so happy.

They'd just left a court hearing regarding custody of his children, for goodness sake. Billy Bob Adams had touched her hair! Ick! Then things had taken a turn for the better. Grady had showed up and gone macho on her behalf. Now he was walking her to her new office and the world looked pretty wonderful. She couldn't get rid of the feeling. But, by God, she was going to try.

"Stop protecting me, Grady."

"Don't look now, but I'm the sheriff. It's my job."

"You'd get no argument from me if I was in danger. But I'm not."

It took a special kind of stupid to say something like that to a man who looked like him. Especially a man who looked like him and also happened to be the sheriff. She'd never seen him in a suit. A look he wore as well or better than any male model in any magazine or catalog she'd ever seen. But now—with his tie at half-mast, his white long-sleeved shirt rolled to his elbows, jacket slung over one shoulder, and reflective sunglasses that hid his eyes— Hubba, hubba. He made her heart do a double back flip that went into a triple spin. And so what if she mixed her sports metaphors?

But how dumb was it to point-blank tell him to cease and desist protecting her?

"What makes you think I'm protecting you?" he said, his brows pulling together in a frown.

She couldn't see the expression behind his sunglasses, but she knew it was there. How? Good question. His tone of voice? Did she know him that well? How could she? There was no answer except that she just did.

"You told me so a few minutes ago."

"Really? What did I say?"

"That you wanted to deck Billy because he touched me."

He stuck the hand not holding his jacket into his slacks pocket. "That doesn't mean I'm protecting you."

"Okay, then what about keeping Zach's secret from me for ten years?"

"That's not just about you. There's no reason the girls need to know."

"It's a tough assignment to protect them from all this."

"I'll figure out a way."

She stopped walking and turned toward him. "It's too sweet for words that you want to. But it may not be in their best interests."

"How can it not?"

"Take it from me. Secrets have a way of coming out at the worst possible time. It might be better to get the situation out in the open, on your terms. Help them deal with it."

"How did keeping secrets hurt you?"

By stealing so many years, she thought. By coming out at a time when she seemed to be waking from an extended period of hibernation. By preventing anything from ever happening with Grady—romantically speaking.

"That's not important," she said, turning away.

She started walking again and he followed. Finally they stopped in front of her empty office.

"So you're my new neighbor," he said.

The space she'd just signed the lease on happened to be right next door to the sheriff's office and across Main Street from Doc Holloway's. The proximity to his place of employment had definitely given her pause. But business sense had muscled its way past her doubts and insecurities. The location was too perfect to pass up. Not to mention the price. Besides, when she'd reported all this to her firm, they'd teased her about needing divine intervention to make the decision.

She smiled brightly at him. "Yup. Howdy, neighbor."

"Aren't you going to show me around?"

''There's nothing to see. It's empty.''

And it was ever so much safer to keep her little flat feet firmly planted out in public on Main Street. What could happen there?

He leaned a hand on the wooden wall just beside her, an in-your-face masculine pose that revved up her pulse. His body was so close she could feel the warmth from his skin, smell the fragrance of his manly no-nonsense soap mixed with the spicy, sexy scent of aftershave. The corners of his mouth turned up, almost as if he sensed her discomfort. As if he was daring her to stand on the street with him and tempt fate.

She and her little flat feet stood corrected. She *did* need protection. From the sheriff! But in the case of Jensen versus the distraction, he had to take some responsibility. He *was* the distraction—with a capital *D*.

''I thought you were going to make a case for why I should put you on my legal team,'' he reminded her.

''You're right. I did say that.''

''Since making a case could take a while, maybe you should invite me inside where it's cooler. Any man one bullet short of a full clip shouldn't be left out in the sun too long.''

Should she point out that based on recent experience being alone with him, inside, away from public consumption of any passerby, was probably not going to be cooler? Nah. That whole thing on her sister's porch had been no more than a fluke. Unlikely to ever happen again.

She pulled a key out of her purse. ''Okay. But like I said, there's no furniture or office equipment yet.''

''What about phones?''

She put the key in the lock and turned it, then

opened the door, leading the way inside. "I'm going to get phone service first thing."

"Good," he said, taking off his sunglasses and sticking them in the pocket of his white shirt. He hung his suit coat on the knob and looked around. "I'd hate to think of you here alone without any means of communication."

"I've got a cell phone," she pointed out.

"Still…"

"There you go again. Protecting me."

"You're habit-forming," he answered, a gleam stealing into his eyes.

Words were her life, but she couldn't think of a single response to his statement. At least, not one that would leave her with even the semblance of dignity.

She swallowed hard. "If I need anything, you're right next door. I'll just holler."

"I'll come running."

Her heart pounded frantically as she tried to catch her breath. One minute she'd been breathing, in-out, in-out, normally. An involuntary function. The next minute—acute oxygen deprivation.

"Okay." She turned away. "I'm sorry there's nowhere for you to sit while I make my case."

"No problem. It won't take long for me to say no."

She whirled around to face him again. She hadn't had a chance to arrange utilities. Without artificial lighting, the interior was dim. But sunlight filtered in from the window, outlining his tall, muscular body. He was too everything—handsome, sort of old-fashioned courtly and sexy as all get-out. Not to mention too darn stubborn for his own darn good.

"Grady, you admitted that my strategy today was

sound. And that was just off the top of my head. Imagine what I could do with research and planning.''

"I'm sure you would be a force to be reckoned with," he answered, looking way down at her.

Now was not the time for tongue-in-cheek humor. One didn't need to have the physical proportions of Stone Cold Steve Austin, the wrestler, to be formidable in court.

"So put me on the team," she pleaded.

"No."

"Ooh, you make me so mad, I could just shake you."

"Not likely."

She stood right in front of him and tapped his chest. "I am your best hope. I'm right under your nose, so to speak. I'm here. I'm handy. I'm very good at what I do." She let out a long breath. "How many ways do I have to say it before you get the message? Why won't you admit it? You *need* me?"

He looked at her for several moments and his eyes smoldered. Then he moved so quickly she didn't have a chance to stop him even if she'd wanted to. Grady curved his hands around her upper arms and pressed her to him, trapping her forearms against his chest. The expression in his blue eyes was fire and ice. A muscle in his lean jaw contracted, testament to his internal struggle.

Without a word, he lowered his mouth to hers. Instead of heat she found his lips cool, firm, yet soft, too. She could almost feel waves of intensity moving through him. Strong, powerful hands held her. He could snap her like a twig, yet his touch was achingly tender. The heady sensation coursed through her like expensive brandy, leaving heat in its wake.

Almost of their own accord, her hands slid up and around his neck. He wrapped his arms around her waist, molding her more firmly to his muscled body. His mouth was magic, cranking up her breathing with soft, hypnotic, nibbling kisses.

She should stop this. It was going to bite her in the backside. But the way her heart skipped and stuttered and soared felt too wonderful. Inside her, rusty feelings stretched, twisted and came to life, giving way to liquid heat. She couldn't find the will to stop herself from sinking farther into his strong embrace. Her breasts flattened against his chest. Could he feel it? Did he know how much she wished he would curve the warmth of his palms over the sensitive peaks?

More delicious sensations burned to life as his tongue swept into her mouth, caressing her. It was like riding a roller coaster, a hairpin curve that left her stomach behind.

She traced the strong line of his neck with one finger, and just the small touch made him suck in his breath and moan. What power. She'd forgotten. Or had she ever really understood?

He pulled his mouth from hers and rested his cheek on her hair as her heart drummed. His chest rose and fell rapidly, evidence of his own breathing difficulties.

"Jen," he murmured, his voice husky and low. Desire vibrated in the single syllable of her name.

In that moment sanity returned. With every fiber of her being she wished it hadn't. But suddenly it was there: he was the legal guardian of children fathered by the man she'd loved.

"Don't," she said, pressing her palms against his chest as he started to lower his head again.

He dropped his hands to his sides. "Why?"

She put her palms flat against his chest and gently pushed. "I can't think with you this close. And I have to think. Because we have to settle things, Grady."

Unfortunately her words lacked a whole lot of conviction. A sensuous haze coursed through her, intoxicating as it went from head to toe. The last thing she wanted was to sober up. But she had to.

He brushed his knuckles across her cheek, then backed up a step. After taking a deep, shuddering breath, he said, "Okay. Shoot."

"You can't ever kiss me again."

"Bull's-eye." His eyes told her he wasn't surprised—or any too happy, either.

"I didn't mean to blurt it out like that. But I only know how to be direct. That's the second time you've kissed me."

"The lady can count."

She ignored his attempt to lighten her up. "There can't be a third time."

"It's the charm, or so the saying goes."

"I appreciate your interest, but I have to be honest with you. A relationship is the last thing I want."

"I thought you said you were being honest." His hand shook as he shoved his fingers through his hair.

"I am."

"All evidence to the contrary. The way you kissed me says you're lying."

"About what?"

"A relationship."

"Look, I won't stand here and say I didn't like it. You're a great kisser."

"Thank you, ma'am," he said, flashing a grin.

Her knees nearly buckled along with her resolve. "But…"

"I hate that word."

"But," she went on, ignoring the interruption, "I had my chance and it didn't work out."

"You know what they say about falling off a horse? You need to get right back on."

"I know where you're going with that and I have to tell you it's an awful lot like the pot calling the kettle black. A guy who's not looking doesn't kiss like that."

His eyebrows went up. "I can see why you're so good at arguing cases in court."

She wasn't the only one. He was doing a darn fine imitation of a man making a case for getting together. Well, this was bad. This made her nervous. She wanted to help him retain custody of his girls, but it meant working closely together. How could she do her best if she had to watch her back—as in worrying that he would kiss her again?

"If I'm good at what I do it's because I pay attention and learn from my mistakes. I learned relationships are a mistake."

"Look, Jen..."

"No, you look, Grady. In law school they taught us it's a really bad idea to become emotionally involved with a client."

"But I'm *not* a client," he pointed out way too reasonably.

"You will be." She folded her arms over her breasts. "I have to be honest with you."

"I'm not sure my fragile ego can take any more honesty."

"There's nothing fragile about you," she said, gazing up, taking in his height. She had to look so far up at him, she could practically go over backward. An exaggeration. But the strength of his shoulders and chest was not. Their power made her think he could hold the weight of the world. But she could easily shatter into a gazillion pieces. "In all honesty, I have to tell you that I'll never care for a man that way again. Not because I'm still in love with Zach," she added hastily.

"Really?"

She nodded. "That ended a long time ago. I found out he wasn't the person I thought."

"I didn't mean to…"

"It wasn't what you told me. I think I knew even before he died."

"Not all men are like him."

"I know. But…" Again she struggled with the words to make him understand. "I'll never forget how *big*—how consuming it was. Love is like a drug. And I've talked to enough kids' counselors to know there's no emotional growth on drugs because they take away all the feelings."

"But you said it—with Zach—was a mistake."

She nodded. It was on the tip of her tongue to tell him about her husband's other women, the nights she'd spent alone wondering where he was, the time he'd slapped her. But there was no point. "I probably would have left him eventually. But I never had to make that decision, because he died. And I shut down."

"Over a man who wasn't worth it."

"Yeah. But at the time I never really faced what he was. Because there was no point. Until now. That means there was no emotional growth."

"It's not too late."

"That's not the point, Grady. I don't want or need

another lesson. If it looks too good to be true, it probably is.''

Who could look better than Grady? He wasn't hard on the eyes. He was a sheriff. And he'd raised, loved and cared for two little girls as if they were his own flesh and blood. Even though he'd known from the beginning they were fathered by a despicable man who'd forced himself on their mother.

And Jen was that man's widow. She'd had the bad judgment to fall for a guy like that. Love was based on respect. How could Grady ever respect a woman like her?

"Jen, I can help you."

"If you truly want to help me, you can add me to your legal team. Let me plan a vigorous defense for your case. You need to let me make sure those two wonderful little girls don't wind up with a despicable person like Billy Bob Adams."

"Jen, I don't know. Why would you put yourself through that?"

"Grady, listen to me. It's not only for you and the girls. It's selfish. *I* need to do this."

"In law school they probably also touched on the downside of taking a case that hits too close to home. Like this one."

She stared at him, trying to decide what to say. It wasn't that she minded obstacles in her path. But why did this obstacle have to be the only man on the planet who actually listened to her? Grady O'Connor was too damn quick for her own good—and don't even get her started on her peace of mind.

She took a deep breath. "The difference is now I know what he did to you. And Lacey. Who knows how things might have been if I hadn't run off with Zach?''

"Don't go there."

"How can I not?" She laced her fingers together and pressed them against her abdomen. "For me this is redemption. It's about righting a wrong that snowballed ten years ago. It's about preventing an even bigger wrong from happening now. Don't you see?''

He looked at her for several moments without answering, then said, "Wow."

"Nonresponsive. Define wow."

"It means I hope I never have to face you on the other side of the aisle in a court of law."

"Is that a yes?''

"When you put it like that, I haven't got an argument left." He nodded. "Welcome aboard, Counselor.''

"You won't be sorry, Grady," she said, then launched herself into his arms.

That instant, automatic, powerful and involuntary response to his yes made Jen hope *she* wouldn't be sorry.

Chapter Seven

A week after giving Jensen the go-ahead to work on his legal problem, Grady paced in front of the picture window in his living room. He watched the long driveway for a flash of BMW red. Jensen had called from her cell phone to say she was on her way home to the Circle S. She had to drive right by his ranch. Could she stop by and talk to him? But her voice had sounded funny.

It was a cell phone, for crying out loud. This was Destiny. Reception was a challenge. So what made him think he could read anything into her tone? His lawman's sixth sense. More than once it had made the hairs on his neck stand up. He'd bet his badge something was wrong. Reception be damned, he'd swear her tone had spooked rabbit written all over it.

Since he had the day off, the girls were home with him. At the moment they were out riding with his foreman, Katherine Lasater. She might be young, but she'd proven her ability and loyalty over and over. He was glad Katie was with them, because his lawman's instincts were screaming that Billy Bob Adams was up to no good today.

Considering her "hands off" ultimatum after he'd kissed her, there was no way Jen would stop by voluntarily. At the time he'd had every intention of playing by her rules. It would be stupid not to.

But now, the sound of her voice on the phone and the memory of having her in his arms combined to skyrocket his pulse. Then her words echoed through his mind as they had countless times since—not a good idea to get involved with a client. She didn't want a relationship. Because of her bad track record.

Okay. Maybe she was right. He could play well with others. And maybe her rules made sense. And what with her warning, he could see a kick in the teeth on his horizon. That wouldn't do him much good.

So what had Billy done to send her running in his direction? Just because her rules made sense didn't mean he couldn't be as happy as a pig in a peach orchard that she was on her way to see him. Grady could almost thank the creep. When he knew Jen was okay, he just might. So he was back to square one and the uneasy tone in her voice. Where the hell was she?

He stopped pacing and glanced out the window. The sight of a cloud of dust, with a sporty red car in front of it, made him breathe a sigh of relief. He walked outside and waited on the covered front porch as she parked in the half-circle drive about fifty feet away. The car door opened and she swung her legs out. This wasn't why he'd stepped outside for a meet and greet. Yeah. And a jury of his peers—men who appreciated the sight of a fantastic pair of female legs—wouldn't convict him for the lie.

He watched her and knew in a hot second when she spotted him. The tension in her body, clued him. And he could see quite a lot of her body thanks to her sundress. It was probably the first time in his life he'd ever been grateful for Texas heat. The hem hit her just above the knee and thin straps curved over her tanned shoulders. The geometric pattern of green and yellow in the dress's fabric made him think of lime sherbet and lemon chiffon pie. Bright, light and fluffy. Jensen was walking, talking sweetness and sunshine. At least, it made him feel that way to look at her.

She waved and smiled, then moved toward him with easy grace. Each step caused her hips to sway and his lust quotient to hike up. A fact he would do his damnedest to keep her from knowing.

He didn't need the message jackhammered into his head. A relationship shouldn't, couldn't, wouldn't and wasn't going to happen.

"Hi, Grady." She walked the three steps up to meet him and slid her sunglasses to the top of her dark hair.

"Hey. C'mon in."

"Thanks. It's a hot one today."

For the sake of his ego, he chose to believe he had something to do with her feeling the heat.

They walked inside and she stopped on the tile foyer to look around. He watched her take in the high, wood-beam ceilings, the living room to the right, formal dining to the left. The entryway formed a *T* at the high wall straight ahead.

"Grady, this is lovely."

"You've been here before."

She shook her head. "No. You must be thinking of someone else. Maybe one of those women you liked and the girls didn't."

"Possible."

She fit into his life so easily, it was hard to believe she'd never been to the ranch before.

"Actually it might have been your sister. I remember Taylor trying to talk me into selling her the dining room set."

Jen lowered the strap of her purse from her shoulder and wrapped it around the small bag, clutching it in her hand. "Obviously she was unsuccessful. Although if I'd been on the negotiating team, it would be on the Circle S. And I wish it was. It's lovely."

He stood beside her, close enough for his long sleeve to lightly brush against her bare arm. Sparks flew, and it might as well have been flesh to flesh. He folded his arms over his chest, forcing his gaze away from her. The ornate mahogany buffet with lighter in-grained wood *was* a beautiful piece of furniture. The large matching table could accommodate all twelve chairs, two of them armchairs, around it.

"This belonged to Lacey's great-grandparents. It's probably a hundred years old."

She walked over and ran a delicate hand reverently over the glossy top and the back of one of the chairs. "It's in excellent shape," she commented.

He was grateful she'd put some distance between them. "Yeah. Some of that good condition is because there haven't been a lot of kids in this house over the years. The women in her family were delicate."

She studied him with an expression of sympathy in her eyes. "I can't even imagine what you went through losing her. Then caring for two baby girls by yourself."

He shrugged. "Her dad and I pulled together. It

gave us an opportunity to bury the hatchet. He was pretty ticked off at me for a while."

"Did he know who the girls' father was?"

He shook his head. "Lacey never wanted him or anyone else to know about that. Until he passed away, her dad and I did pretty well with the twins."

"Now I guess it's tough being mother *and* father to two girls on the brink of being teenagers."

"Yeah. I don't know a whole lot about being a mother, and that makes being a father to two growing girls harder every day."

"I bet you still miss Lacey a lot."

Grady met Jen's gaze and wondered what she was thinking. There was a spark in her eyes, making him wonder if she hoped she was wrong about it. Then he remembered her asking him the same question the last night of the championships, and he hadn't exactly answered her. He still didn't quite know how to respond. Or did he just not want her to know the truth?

"I wish she'd lived to see the girls grow up," he finally said.

She put her hand on his arm. "You're not worried that the girls may be too delicate, are you?"

"I worry about them in every way possible."

The corners of her mouth curved up. "Let me rephrase the question. Medicine is advancing constantly. When they have children—"

"And we hope it's not premature—you'll pardon the pun." His heart slammed against the wall of his chest when she smiled.

"That goes without saying. But when all the factors are in place and the time is right for them to be moms, I'm sure your girls will do fine."

"What about you? Are you fine?"

"I don't expect I'll ever have children."

The statement made him damn curious, but he wasn't going to ask. She'd made it clear her personal life was none of his concern. "That's not what I meant. When you called, it sounded like something was wrong."

Surprise widened her green eyes. "All I said was I've got some things to discuss with you. Do you mind if I come over?"

"You said *right over*. Big difference."

"Since I was close, it was the appropriate thing to say. But next time I'll be careful how I phrase it when I invite myself over."

"So there's nothing wrong."

"Actually there is something. Not exactly wrong. And I was trying not to alarm you."

"What is it?" He studied her, even more closely, if possible. "Billy?"

She nodded. "He came to my office."

"Did he hurt you? If he did, I swear I'll..." Instantaneous fury coursed through him at the idea of Jen being hurt. The power of the feeling rocked him.

"I'm fine, Grady," she said, putting her hand on his arm again as if to hold him back. "Although the proximity of my office to yours didn't do me a whole lot of good with you not in town."

He let out a relieved breath. "I took the day off. But there are deputies on duty. You could have hollered." He covered her hand and found it cold. Wrapping her fingers in his warm ones, he was pleased when she didn't pull away.

"There was no need to holler. I handled it. But I'll admit that guy gives me the willies."

"What did he say?"

Her gaze clouded. "Let's just say you were right about him wanting something. Besides the girls, I mean."

"Is it just you, or do all lawyers take a hundred words to say what they could spit out in two?"

"Is there somewhere we can sit down and talk about this?"

He smiled, and tension drained out of him. Obviously she was fine. "Sure. Sorry. I guess the idea of him threatening you put me off my manners."

"He didn't actually threaten me."

"I don't like the sound of that."

"Don't get your white hat in a twist, hero. I'm fine, and heaven forbid you should forget your manners."

A reluctant grin turned up the corners of his mouth. "Okay. Let's go in the kitchen. Have you had lunch yet?"

"Lunch?" She pulled her hand from his to look at her watch, making him miss the contact. "It's way past lunchtime. Besides, I don't want to impose. What I need to talk to you about won't take long. I just meant to—"

"I haven't had lunch yet. And I'm talking sandwich, nothing more." Although the look on her face said she was worried about the "more" part.

"I never intended to take up much of your time."

He'd known her visit was all about business. Until she shut him down just now, he hadn't realized he was hoping to change her mind about it. The disappointment took him by surprise. Or maybe it was the wanting her visit to be a little bit about him. Either way, nothing changed. She wasn't here on his account.

"Well, I haven't eaten yet, and I'm starved," he said, unable to prevent a quick glance at her lush lips.

"Let's go in the kitchen. The least I can do is pour you a glass of something cold while you give me the bad news about Billy."

"If you offer me a beer, I swear I'm outta here," she warned.

He knew she was remembering Billy's offer on the steps of the courthouse. "Nothing more dangerous than sweet tea is what I had in mind. Follow me."

Instinctively he took her hand and led her to the foyer's dead end, then turned right. They passed through the family room to the kitchen at the back of the house. He couldn't help wondering if a sophisticated attorney like herself would like the country decor. Not fancy, but then comfort was the goal.

A leather sofa and matching love seat sat at a right angle to each other in front of a large-screen TV and stereo system. A stone fireplace with raised hearth took up the better part of one wall. Kasey and Stacey had left softball mitts and bats on the floor along with books, comics, dolls, stuffed animals and various pens, pencils, crayons and paper. Through the long row of windows the Texas prairie stretched as far as the eye could see.

"This is very homey," Jen commented.

"Is that a diplomatic way of saying I need a housekeeper?"

She laughed. "No. It was an honest statement of my feelings."

"Okay. We like it. And as soon as the girls get back from their ride, they've got some chores to do."

He walked into the kitchen with her hand still in his, feeling as right as could be. "Here we are."

"This is nice," she said, looking around as if she might be impressed.

"It was remodeled before Lacey's dad died." Reluctantly he let her hand go.

The large room had an island in the center with a nook at the far end holding a big pine table and six matching chairs. A cooktop was set in the countertop and a combination built-in oven and microwave took up space on one wall. He put his hand on the refrigerator handle just inside the doorway.

"Soda or iced tea?" he asked.

"Just water."

He nodded and grabbed a glass from the oak cupboard and filled it with ice and water. "Here."

"Thanks," she said, taking it from him.

Their fingers brushed, even though she obviously tried to avoid touching him. Her glance darted to his and twin spots of color stained the smooth skin of her cheeks. After putting her purse down, she leaned her elbows on the island.

"So tell me what Billy Bob Adams is up to now." He folded his arms across his chest and leaned back against the ceramic-tile countertop beside the refrigerator. Only the island separated them. For all the good it did him, it might as well have been the real thing surrounded by water.

She took a sip of water, then tucked a strand of hair behind her ear. "He hinted that he would drop the lawsuit if you made it worth his while."

"Essentially selling the kids?"

She nodded. "That's not all. He implied that he might tell the girls the whole ugly story about their biological father if you don't give him something to change his mind."

"Damn it. Son of a..." He stopped and let out a long breath. "What did you say?"

"I bluffed. At least, I think I did. Have you explained anything to the girls yet about what's going on?"

"No."

"Then I definitely bluffed. I told him to go right ahead."

"For God's sake, Jen. What were you thinking?"

"First of all, that I didn't like being alone with him. Second, that there's no way you're going to let that creep near enough to the girls for him to tell them boo. And third, if I could convince him they already knew, he'd have nothing to gain. I also warned him that blackmail and extortion are illegal."

"Did he have a reaction?"

"Oh, yeah. Apparently I'm not a very good bluffer, because he said he didn't believe me and indicated he would be willing to keep everything to himself for the right amount of money."

"What did you say?"

"I told him you don't have a lot of liquid cash. Everything is tied up in the ranch."

"Then what happened?"

"He laughed. So I gave him a pen and paper and told him to write down a number."

"You're kidding."

"Nope. I'm serious. Then I gave him a drink of water in a glass in case my pen wasn't big enough to get a good set of fingerprints." She opened her purse and pulled out a pen and a glass in a plastic bag. "I thought you and Jack might be able to use these."

Grady grinned. "Way to go, Counselor. Then what did you do?"

"I threw him out of my office."

"Literally?"

"I asked him politely to get his backside out before I called the sheriff. *That* part was a bluff because, of course, we both know you weren't there."

He couldn't help smiling at the idea of her throwing any guy out. Little thing like her? Not happening in this lifetime. Then the reality of the situation sank in yet again. "Shouldn't that information be enough to take to the judge to get this whole thing thrown out of court?"

"In a perfect world it would be." She sighed.

"I hear a but."

"It's not that easy."

"Easy?" he asked skeptically.

"Okay. None of this is easy. I should have said the legalities aren't cut-and-dried. His language was vague, the threats couched in generalities. It would be my word against his and it could easily be argued that my word in this case is compromised. Due to the fact that I'm representing his opposition."

"So we know he doesn't want the kids, but there's no way to prove it?"

"That about sums it up." She met his gaze. "I thought you were going to have a sandwich."

"I just lost my appetite. Is that all the news you wanted to deliver?"

"No. I've got an appointment for you and the girls tomorrow with Hannah Morgan. She's going to take buccal swabs on all of you."

"What's that?"

"She's going to dab the inside of your mouths and send the swabs to an independent lab for DNA testing."

He sighed. "Is that everything?"

"Yeah. What can I say? The wheels of justice are square."

"Meaning?"

"We have to take this one step at a time. Leave nothing to chance." She took another sip of water. "You need to prepare the girls for what's going to happen."

"I thought I'd tell them it's part of their yearly physical. Since Hannah's filling in for Doc Holloway, I was hoping they'd figure the whole thing is just a difference in doctors."

"Oh, Grady, they're way too smart for that. You have to explain what's going on, what's going to happen. You know, they really do need to know the truth. There could be medical issues, if nothing else."

"I know."

"You don't want them to find out and be shocked. What if they hear something in town? You know nothing stays a secret long in Destiny."

"Yeah."

Except the ten-year-old secret that her husband was the father of his girls. Grady studied her, the genuine concern on her face. The look tugged at his heart. What if they fell in love? Grady and Jensen. The two of them head over heels?

Even if she would admit to having feelings for him, what if she couldn't get past the fact that Zach had fathered his girls? She'd been great with them at the rodeo, but that was before she'd learned the truth. Would she still be so good with them? If not, how could he have a relationship with a woman who couldn't accept his children? And Jen had reason enough to turn her back on them—walking, talking reminders of the pain she was trying to forget.

But talk about jumping the gun. He had nothing to worry about. The last thing she wanted was a relationship. She'd said it straight out; she was putting up all the roadblocks. In spite of her protest that she'd made a mistake and probably wouldn't have stayed with Zach, Grady didn't completely buy it. Or the fact that she no longer loved the man she'd married and lost.

Grady believed she now knew Zach wasn't the guy she'd thought. But as the town sheriff, he'd seen smart women make the same mistake over and over. It was called dysfunctional, and domestic violence was the result. She and Zach had never gotten a chance to get that far, so Jen had never seen the violent side of him. And she'd had ten years to remember only the good stuff. That was a roadblock he didn't think he could hurdle.

The hell of it was, he was damned attracted to her. Maybe for the first time in his life he was thinking about a lifetime with one woman. His own happily ever after. It was a chance he might be willing to take. If she felt half of what he did, she'd be willing, too. But she'd shut him down. That meant she must still be carrying a torch for Zach.

"Grady?"

He felt a hand on his arm, and gazed into a pair of pretty green eyes. Correction: pretty, worried green eyes.

"Hmm?"

"You zoned out."

"Yeah. I've got some things on my mind."

"Of course." She set her half-full glass of water on the counter beside him. "That's my cue to leave."

When he wanted her to stay so badly, the last thing

he'd do was give her a reason to go. But maybe it was for the best. No point in beating his head against the wall.

"What time did you say the appointment is? With Dr. Morgan?"

"Two o'clock. First one after lunch."

"Okay."

"Do you want me to help you talk to the girls? Prepare them?"

He shook his head. "I'll take care of it."

He needed her legal expertise. But that was business. No way would he make it personal. Counting on Jensen Stevens wasn't something he needed to get used to.

Chapter Eight

While staring intently at her computer screen, Jen heard the whisper of her office door opening. A warm breeze darting in from outside fluttered her hair and she glanced up. Then did a double take. Kasey and Stacey O'Connor stood in front of her, each of them holding some kind of ceramic figure in their arms.

"Hi, Jensen," one of them said.

Was it Stacey or Kasey? Until one of them brushed the hair off their forehead to show the scar or lack of one, she couldn't tell.

"H-hi," she said, swiveling her chair away from the computer to face them.

When she'd met the twins at the championships, she'd been captivated. They were completely adorable. But this was the first time she'd seen them since learning that Zach was their biological father. She was suddenly and completely nervous.

The two little faces—solemn big brown eyes, turned-up noses splashed with freckles, and full

mouths with a lovely and very defined upper lip—
were identical. They had the same shade of golden-
blond hair. But they couldn't have been dressed more
differently. One in denim shorts, a T-shirt and sneak-
ers. The other wearing a frilly pink sundress and white
sandals. One adjusted her baseball hat, turning the bill
backward to reveal a scar at her hairline. Okay. Now
she was getting somewhere. Thank goodness Grady
didn't dress them in identical outfits. He let them express their individuality. Stacey was the tomboy.

Jen guessed the baseball equipment she'd seen
strewn around Grady's family room the day before
belonged to Stacey. Did she just like sports? Or was
she very athletic? Zach had been a national champion
bull rider before he was killed. Had both girls inherited
their father's ability? She meant Zach. Grady was their
father. Good Lord, this was awkward—and confusing.
Fortunately she hadn't said any of that out loud. But
the two girls continued to stare at her. And the stare
was turning into puppy-dog eyes.

She folded her hands together and rested them on
her desk. "Does your dad know where you are?"

Stacey glanced at her sister. When she looked back,
she had an answer. "He brought us to town."

Did the two of them have telepathy? ESP? She'd
heard communication between twins could border on
extrasensory.

"Where is he? Your dad," she clarified.

"In his office," they said together.

"Where are you supposed to be?"

Two sets of thin shoulders rose in a shrug. Nonresponsive. Grady was the overprotective type under the
best of circumstances, and lately circumstances had
been downright lousy. She would bet her Beemer he

didn't know these two had slipped next door without permission. Was that the beginnings of a wild streak? Maybe a trait they'd gotten from Zach? Did they have traces of their biological father? How big a role did environment play in raising good kids? Or was this just a response to their world turning upside down? Grady had probably talked to them yesterday just as he'd said he would.

She shook her head. This whole train of thought was a wreck waiting to happen. Not to mention counter-productive. The man she'd married hadn't been perfect and he'd kept parts of his personality hidden from her. But he wasn't a monster. She'd have seen if he were and never would have loved him. Still, it was oddly comforting that the twins' physical appearance favored their mother.

"You're supposed to be with your dad in his office, aren't you?"

The two looked at each other again, somehow assessing whether or not to come clean. Meeting her gaze again, they'd apparently decided to cut their losses. "We *had* to see you," Kasey volunteered dramatically.

"It's really important, Jensen," Stacey added.

"Okay. What can I do for you?"

The girls put the ceramic figures on her desk. Studying them more closely, she realized the things were shaped like pigs and had a slit in the top for coins. They were piggy banks. What the heck was going on?

"Girls," she said, looking at each in turn, "you're going to have to tell me what you want."

Stacey said, "We want to hire you for our lawyer."

Jen was glad her chair sat firmly beneath her fanny. If she'd been standing, the shock of that statement could have landed her on the floor. Struggling not to show them the reaction, she smiled.

"Okay. Why?"

"Daddy talked to us."

Good. Grady O'Connor was a man of his word. A *brave* man of his word to discuss the situation with two little girls all by himself. But she needed to know what words he'd used with them.

Always best not to jump in with both feet, especially when there could be quicksand. Get all the info possible before digging herself in deeper. Or let something slip. She couldn't assume he'd discussed the lawsuit with them. "What did your dad say?"

Kasey glanced at her sister. "Stuff."

Jen's mouth twitched and she wanted to laugh at this comic exchange. But she managed to maintain a serious expression she hoped matched theirs. For one to gather information, it had to be available and relatively specific. "Stuff" took in a lot of territory.

"Could you be more precise? Tell me exactly what your dad said?"

One shoulder beneath the strap of Kasey's pink sundress went up.

Stacey wasn't so taciturn. "He said he's not our dad. He said our real dad's brother wants to take us away from him. He said we got an appointment with some lady doctor today and she's gonna gag us with a cotton ball on a stick." When she stopped, her chin trembled.

That did it. Jen stood and rounded her desk. She didn't ordinarily make a habit of hugging her clients. But, damn it, this was different.

The girls molded themselves to her—one on each side, with their arms squeezing her waist. She put her arms around them, hugging them back as tightly as she could. No matter what, they were children. Confused about what was going on. Darn it, she wished Grady had let her be there when he'd talked to them. But she couldn't really blame him. Because of who she was—who she'd married.

She squeezed their shoulders. "What do you want to know, girls?"

"Is that man our uncle?" Stacey's hat fell off when she looked up. "Is our dad really our dad?"

"Can you remember what Grady—your dad—said?" How much had he told them? Had he said anything about how they were conceived?

"He said we were in Mommy's tummy when he married her. That man who's our real uncle asked the judge to make us live with him but he—the sheriff—won't let that happen."

"But we don't know if he's our real dad or not," Kasey said. "So Stacey said we should ask you. But *I* said lawyers cost a lot of money. I saw that on TV. So we got our piggy banks. Together we have eight dollars and sixty-seven cents. It would be more, but we spent our allowance on squirt guns. Is that enough for a lawyer?"

"Yes." As tears blurred her eyes, Jen squeezed the twins close again. "You're in luck. This office just opened and I've got a special offer going. Free consultation."

Two identical foreheads wrinkled with confusion. "What's that?" they both asked.

"It's when you get to ask me any questions you want, for as long as you want. No charge."

Their faces brightened. "Wow."

Jen sat on one of the metal-framed, plastic-covered

chairs she'd placed in front of her desk for clients. Eventually she planned to upgrade. She tugged Kasey onto her lap and put her arm around Stacey, snuggling the little girl against her side. "So ask away. Anything. As many questions as you want."

The small, sturdy bodies in her arms made her feel warm from the inside out. The sensation was amazingly wonderful. These bright, beautiful, terrific little girls filled her with love—just because they were children. They needed her. And she needed to be needed.

Kasey smoothed her dress over her knees. "The most important thing we want to know is—who's our real dad?"

Jensen looked from one to the other. "Do you guys know what an officer of the court is?"

Identical blank looks settled over their faces. "Is it like being a sheriff?"

Jensen shook her head. "Not exactly. But it's part of being a lawyer and it means I have to tell the truth. Okay?"

"Okay," they said together.

The clouds lifted from their serious little faces and twin smiles were her reward. She could rack up a gazillion billable hours for her legal services and it would never be as satisfying as putting to rest the fears and insecurities of these two little girls.

"What about that man? That guy who says he's our uncle?" Stacey asked.

Jen looked from one girl to the other. "He's trying to get the judge to give him custody—that means he wants you to live with him."

"Would we have to go away?" Stacey wanted to know.

Jen shook her head. "In my opinion, no." That was

an educated guess. Billy Bob wanted the ranch, and getting physical custody of the girls was the only way he could accomplish it.

Stacey nodded. "Good. Because I don't want to leave Destiny. I've got a lot of friends on my baseball team."

"I've got a lot of friends, too," Kasey said.

"I bet you do," Jen answered. "Don't worry, you guys. Your dad and I are going to do whatever it takes to keep everything just the way it is."

"Do we hafta get our mouth washed out with the cotton stick?"

"I'll tell you exactly what's going to happen." She adjusted her hold on the girls. "Dr. Hannah Morgan is going to take a swab—it's like a cotton ball on a stick—but she's not going to gag you. It's not like when you have a sore throat. She'll rub it gently on the inside of each of your mouths. That's it. It won't hurt. I promise it's really easy."

"Why?"

"She's going to send it to a lab where they run tests on it that will show who your father is."

"But the sheriff said our bye-logical father is dead."

She nodded. "That's true. He was a bull rider and died in a rodeo accident."

"How can the doctor test him?"

She hesitated for a moment, then decided the truth was always best. "I was married to your biological father."

The two faces brightened. "Then you're practically our mother."

"No." Although part of her wished she was. "But I'm your friend. The point is, I've got some things of his—a lock of his hair—that can be tested. The results will prove that he's your father. But that's not always the most important thing to a judge. She's going to take into account your home environment, you have a nice house, clean clothes, enough to eat, the fact that you're both good girls who never get into trouble.''

Stacey frowned. ''Will the judge send me away because I threw a water balloon at Logan Peterson? I did it because he pushed my sister. The counselor at camp said it was bad and I should use words. I had to write a hundred times 'I will not throw water balloons.'''

''No.'' Jen shook her head for emphasis. ''That's normal kid stuff.''

''That's a relief.'' Stacey put her arm around Jen's neck. ''Next time I'll throw a rock at him. That's not so much to write.''

Behind her, the door opening stopped her ''that wouldn't be a good idea'' speech. Then a long, broad shadow crawled up the wall in front of her. Somehow she knew who was there, and a warm feeling poured through her that had nothing to do with the girls and everything to do with their father. But he would have to wait. This conversation couldn't.

''Do you know who our real father is?'' Stacey asked again.

''You bet I do,'' she answered.

''But what about the test?'' Kasey wanted to know.

''The DNA will tell who your biological father is. But I don't need any old DNA test to know who your real dad is.'' Jen looked from one earnest face to the other.

She wondered about Zach. If he'd lived, would he have acknowledged them? He'd known of the pregnancy, but never bothered to take things a step further and claim them. But he'd traveled all over the country. He'd been young—

The thought stopped her. Grady had been exactly the same age when he'd assumed responsibility for identical twin infant girls not his own. What an awesome, difficult undertaking. To do something so selfless he must have loved their mother a lot. Lacey hadn't lived a long life, but she'd known a lifetime of love. What would it be like to have that kind of love from a man? A man like Grady O'Connor? Her heart pounded and she held in the threatening sigh.

Stacey patted the hand at her waist. "So who is it, Jensen? Who's our real dad?"

"Grady O'Connor is your real father in every single way that's important," she said emphatically.

"Well, now…"

Guiltily, the girls jumped away from her and whirled around. "Hi, Dad," they said together.

"I was worried about you guys," he said.

"We didn't mean to worry you," Stacey said. "We just needed a lawyer. We had questions."

He opened his arms wide and they went to him, one on each side. He squatted down and nestled them close, taking in a deep breath.

He met her gaze. Humor evaporated the concern in his eyes. "Did you get them all answered?" he asked them.

"If not," Jen said, "there's still time. The free offer is still good."

"Offer?" he asked.

"Grand opening special," she explained. "Free consultation."

The sight of him turned her brain to mush. She was surprised she got out words of more than one syllable.

Consultation was a real challenge. Especially when the spark in his eyes told her he was pleased about what she'd said to the girls. She wished there was a law against her growing feelings for this man. Number one: he wasn't likely to feel any respect for the woman who'd married the man responsible for what he was going through now. But the cold dose of reality didn't put the brakes on her attraction. Number two: she had a very important job to do. Distraction from a six-foot hunk and a half wouldn't help to win his case.

Number three: there was no number three. When she put an end to his legal troubles, there would be no need for them to have contact. She wouldn't give him an opportunity to tell her to her face that he could never love the woman who'd had the bad judgment to marry Zach—even though that judgment had been young and stupid.

But watching him with the girls made her loneliness more acute. An aching void the size of Texas opened up inside her. She wished she could be a part of that warmth and love. Realization hit her between the eyes. These girls had captivated her from the first. The truth about their conception couldn't change her feelings.

Kasey tugged on his shirt. "Daddy, we're hungry. Can we go to lunch at the Road Kill Café before we hafta go to the doctor?"

"Sure, squirt."

"Daddy, can Jensen come with us?" Stacey begged.

He looked at Jensen. "Would you care to join us, Counselor? My treat. To say thanks for your free consultation."

Jen's heart skipped. Say no, her sensible self warned. No. No. No. She looked into his eyes and the

word *no* was on the tip of her tongue. Then Grady
grinned and took the starch right out of her backbone.

She nodded. "Thanks. I'd love to go with you."

"Yaay," the girls cheered, breaking away from
their father. They grabbed her hands and pulled her to
her feet. "Let's go."

Jen was going, all right. Straight to hell in a hand-
basket.

The twins poked around in the toothpicks and mints
by the café cash register. Grady had given them the
lunch bill and the money to pay while he and Jen
stayed in the booth. The two kids needed to expend
restless energy and this gave him a chance to spend a
little more time with her—alone.

She looked at him across the red-and-white check-
ered tablecloth littered with the remains of their meal.
"You really should let me get my own lunch."

"You didn't order enough to keep a bird alive. And
you hardly touched what you *did* order. Besides, I already promised to buy."

"I don't feel right about this. But at least I'm a
cheap date," she said.

"Date?" One eyebrow lifted in question.

"You know what I meant."

"Yeah."

Nothing personal. He'd gotten the message. But
seeing how great she'd been with the twins, and
spending time together—the four of them—the message was getting less and less clear. Especially after
what she'd said, confirming he was their father in
every way.

Grady rested his arm on the leather-covered booth
back. "I want to thank you."

"Why?" she asked, tilting her head slightly.

"For what you said to the girls in your office. I talked to them but—"

"They told me. Really, Grady. Gag them with a cotton stick?"

One corner of his mouth rose. "That's not what I told them."

"It's what they heard."

"That's not my fault. Although I appreciate you clearing up their questions."

"You're welcome."

"Especially the one about who their real father is."

"That's a no-brainer," she said. "It's the guy who walked the floor with them when they were babies. Changed their diapers. Puts food on the table. Tucks them in bed at night." She smiled. "You. I just told them the Lord's honest truth."

"Yeah, well, they've taken a shine to you, Miss Stevens."

She looked surprised. Pleased, but surprised. "How can you tell?"

"Are you fishing for compliments?"

"If I put bait on my line, I expect to reel something in. You bet I'm fishing for compliments."

"Why do you think they went to you for clarification of what I told them?" He thought for a minute. Back to that last night of the high school rodeo championships. When she'd hung out with the girls in the bleachers. "You can braid hair and you bought them all the junk food they could eat. What's not to like?"

"My taste in men."

"Zach."

It wasn't a question, but she nodded. "I was so clueless."

"They say love is blind."

"Do they say it's dumb, too?" she asked, a tinge of bitterness in her tone.

"You can't beat yourself up over it, Jen. That was a long time ago."

"Feels like yesterday. What is it about coming back to Destiny now? It feels like the past is catching up."

"Maybe it's time. So we can put it to rest."

At that moment the girls ran over. "Is it time to go to the doctor?"

Grady slid out of the booth. "Yes."

"Are you coming with us, Jensen?" Stacey asked.

She nodded. "I have to take a sample to the doctor, too."

They walked outside and the girls skipped ahead on the wooden sidewalk. Only Maggie Benson's shop, This 'n That, separated the café from Doc Holloway's office.

He wished she didn't have anything that belonged to her husband. To hang on to mementos implied she still cared. Grady didn't want her to have leftover feelings for the guy. He didn't deserve it. But more important, Jen deserved more.

They ambled slowly toward their destination. He watched the girls disappear safely inside the doctor's office. Even though he knew this was merely a formality, he wasn't crazy about this.

"I talked to Jack Riley," he said. "We're running a search on the fingerprints."

"Anything?" she asked hopefully.

He shook his head. "Not yet, but he only got them this morning."

"In case it's a dead end, I'll have to come up with Plan B."

"It's not enough that I'm a good father?"

"You'll get a chance to prove that in court."

"I prove it every day—in real life."

"I know. And we'll make sure the court knows, too." She slipped her hand into the bend of his elbow and snuggled in for a sort of sideways hug. "You have to be patient. We'll win this, Grady."

"If you say so." It felt too damn good to have her this close to him and he wished they were anywhere except Main Street, Destiny. "After all, you're my kids' lawyer and you have to tell them the truth."

"Here we are," she said, stopping in front of the doctor's office.

In the half-glass door was etched Frank Holloway, M.D.

Grady pushed it open for her. "Lawyers first."

"I thought it was ladies," she said, her lips curving up.

"It would be if we weren't here for DNA tests."

They walked up to the counter, where two glass doors hid the reception desk. Grady knocked softly and the door was instantly opened.

"Hey, Sheriff."

"Addie."

Addie Ledbetter had bright blue eyes and even brighter red hair. She looked like the title character from an episode of *I Love Lucy,* only twenty pounds heavier.

"We've got everything set up for you."

Grady rested his hands on the counter. "Has Billy Adams been here?"

The frown on the office nurse's face gave him his answer. "There's something not quite right about that guy."

Jen sniffed. "You can say that again."

"Once is enough. And that means I hope I never lay eyes on him in this office again." She angled her head toward the hall. "Doc Morgan is with the girls in exam room one. You can go on back."

"Thanks, Addie," Grady said.

He opened the back office door and let Jen precede him through it. Without a word they walked down the carpeted hall, glancing at the neutral-colored prints lining the walls. When they entered the room, he saw Hannah swabbing Stacey's mouth. The doctor then did the same to Kasey. Each swab was placed in a plastic tube labeled with the appropriate name.

"Okay, you guys can go pick out a toy. Do you know where Doc keeps them?" Hannah asked.

"Yup. Hi, dad. Hi, Jen." The girls raced past him and out of the room.

He watched them hurry down the hallway, then looked back in the room. "Hi, Hannah,"

The blond, blue-eyed doctor turned to him and smiled. "Sheriff." The look she slid to Jen had curious written all over it.

"This is Jensen Stevens," he said, introducing the two women. "Our attorney."

She held out her hand. "You're Taylor's sister. I remember you from high school."

"You went to Destiny High?" Jen asked.

She nodded. "I'm not surprised you don't remember me. I skipped a couple grades and was into geek stuff, major nerd mode."

"And look where you are now." Jen smiled. "It's nice to meet you, Hannah."

"Same here. Especially after what the twins said. It

was Jensen this. And Jensen that. You're the best thing since sliced bread.''

''If only the partners in my law firm were as easy as those two. They're complete sweethearts.''

''I couldn't agree more.'' She looked up at Grady. ''Okay, big guy. It's your turn. Hop up on the table. I'll be gentle with you. This won't hurt a bit.''

''That's what all the pretty ladies say.'' All except Jensen, he thought. And he realized she was the one he wanted to hear it from.

But he did as he was told and opened wide when ordered. It took less than a second and he was finished.

Hannah turned to Jensen. ''I understand you've got something from your husband that has to go to the lab?'' Hannah took off her disposable gloves, toed open the lid on the metallic trash can and tossed them in.

Jen pulled a plastic bag from her purse. ''Here. It's a lock of Zach's hair. I found it in a scrapbook stored at my sister's ranch.''

Hannah took it and nodded. ''I'll get all of these in the mail this afternoon—''

''In my experience results usually come back in about ten days if the lab's not backed up,'' Jen said.

''To be honest, I haven't any experience with this sort of testing,'' Hannah admitted.

Jen's face tensed into her lawyer expression. ''Look, Doctor—''

''Hannah, please.''

''Okay, Hannah. I'm going to be honest with you. There aren't going to be any DNA surprises. But we want as much time as we can get to plan a strategy. Would it hurt anything to hold off mailing these samples till tomorrow? Or the next day—''

"Or the day after that?" Hannah asked, smiling.

Jen grinned. "I see we're on the same page."

"I know what's going on," the doctor admitted. "Normally I don't make snap judgments about people, but Billy Bob Adams made my skin crawl. There's no way he should get within ten feet of those girls. If I can help by sending those samples out by pony express, consider it done."

"Thanks." Jen glanced at Grady. "It's quite obvious the woman is gifted."

"Destiny gossip says Dev Hart thinks so, too," Grady commented.

"We're just old friends." The color flooding the doctor's face said something completely different.

"That's what all the pretty ladies say." Again he meant Jen. But they were definitely on different pages. He wanted more than friendship. "I better go get the girls. Thanks, Doc."

They went out to the waiting room, where the twins were watching fish swim in the aquarium in the corner. When Grady and Jensen walked up behind them, the girls turned.

"Dad, Kasey and me been thinking..."

"A dangerous thing," he said to Jen.

"Don't make fun, Daddy," Kasey said. "This is serious."

"Okay." He put on his thoughtful expression. "What have you been thinking?"

"First we have a question."

"Shoot," he said.

"It's for Jensen."

She stepped up beside him. "Shoot."

Stacey adjusted her baseball hat. "Would we have

a better chance of staying with our dad if he was married?''

In spite of the fact that her cheeks were pink, Jen met his gaze. One of his eyebrows rose in question. ''I don't know for sure,'' she hedged.

''Guess,'' they ordered her.

''Okay. I'd have to say with two single men wanting custody of you guys, one a biological relative, the other your dad in every way but—if he had a wife it would probably tip the scales in his favor.''

''That's what we thought,'' Stacey said. The two girls looked at each other and smiled. ''We have the perfect solution, Daddy. You should marry Jensen.''

Chapter Nine

Jen looked from the satisfied expressions of the two little girls to the surprised yet amused face of their father, a peace officer who didn't do a thing for *her* peace—of mind.

"I don't quite know what to say," she answered.

"That's bad," Grady commented. "A lawyer should never be at a loss for words."

"Tell me about it."

"Just say yes," Stacey advised. "It's not drugs or anything, so you don't hafta say no."

Grady O'Connor was like a drug and she was finding it harder every day to say no.

With difficulty, Jen concentrated. "Somewhere in that statement is logic. I'm just not sure where."

"Oh, Jen," Kasey said, clapping her hands together, "it's brilliant."

"Beyond brilliant," her sister added.

"Your father hasn't asked me," she said, hoping that would put an end to the matter. Because the fact of the matter was he wouldn't want her. Her stomach knotted. She couldn't look at him, because she was afraid she would see in his eyes that she was right.

"But you love our dad, right?" Stacey asked. "Everybody in town loves our dad."

The hits just kept on coming. "Your dad is a fine man, but I...we... It's not that simple, girls. Two people shouldn't get married *unless* they love each other. It's the first, best and only reason."

At that moment she glanced at Grady. He had the oddest expression on his face.

"Right, Sheriff?" she asked him.

"Right." His tone lacked conviction.

She ignored him and looked at the girls. Bending to their eye level, she rested her hands on her knees. She decided to leave out the part where she hoped to prove that their uncle was unfit for fatherhood. Accentuate the positive.

"You guys have to trust me. It's my job to convince the judge that staying with your dad is the best thing for you."

"How?" Stacey asked.

"I need to show the court that he has wings, a halo and can walk on water."

"Is that good?" both girls questioned, clearly confused by her choice of words.

"It means I'm practically a saint," their dad explained.

Kasey blinked as her long bangs caught in her eyelashes. She brushed them aside. "How are you going to show the judge our dad is the best?"

Jen slid a glance to the self-satisfied lawman in question and made a mental note to get him a new hat—in a size that would accommodate his rapidly expanding ego.

"He's the sheriff," she pointed out, as if that explained everything. Two pairs of blank brown eyes stared back at her. "At the same time he's running a flourishing ranch. He's raising you girls by himself and doing a great job. You're terrific. He's a pillar of the community. So you see, there's nothing to worry about."

Right. For them. She, on the other hand, had a lot to worry about. She'd done such a good job convincing them their dad was the best thing since the electric light bulb, her own heart believed it too well. She was doing her best to resist him and failing miserably. But she could never mean as much to him as Lacey.

Jen knew her road to romance had dead-ended ten years ago. She hadn't out-and-out-lied when asked if she loved their dad. Her officer-of-the-court status was intact. Barely. As far as falling for him, she was sliding out of control and trying to get a handhold to stop her descent. If she could just do that, she'd worry about climbing out of the pit later. Distance. She needed it now and the more the better.

"Let me walk you back to your office," she said to him.

He nodded. "And I'll walk you back to yours."

So, the distance strategy needed some work. Whatever had possessed her to lease space next door to him?

He tapped each of his daughters on their turned-up, freckled noses. "Then I have to take these two to day camp at the park."

Stacey looked at her twin. "Race you to the sheriff's office.'' She was gone before her sister could answer.

Kasey looked at Jensen, then Grady. "Daddy, I still think marrying Jensen is the best idea.'' Then she took off after her sister.

Leaving Jen alone with their father.

"Well," she said.

"Eloquent, yet deep.'' The look on his face was so completely cute.

Distance. She needed to get away from him. Wait. She'd already realized proximity wasn't the answer, since their offices were side by side. She was bound to run into him. Often. That left her only one alternative. Work. She needed work. And lots of it.

Jen glanced at the clock on her wall. Six forty-five in the evening. She turned off her computer, then rubbed her eyes. It was time to go home. Or rather to Taylor's. Where her sister and Mitch were deliriously in love. Jen couldn't be happier.

Or sadder. For herself. She really needed to find a place of her own. She'd moved her things from her Dallas apartment and it was time to give Mitch and Taylor privacy. After all, they would be married soon.

As she stood and stretched, she looked through her office window at the couple outside on the walkway. Maggie Benson's red curls were hard to miss. Not to mention Jack Riley, black-haired, blue-eyed hunk that he was.

When he noticed her, he waved, then opened her door. "Hey, Jen."

"Jack," she said, smiling. "How's it going?"

"Never better."

Maggie slid around in front of him. "Hi. Looks like

you're wrapping up for the day. Want to join us for dinner?''

''Where's Faith?''

''Sleepover with a friend. What do you say? I'm dying to tell you all about our wedding plans.''

Jen groaned inwardly at the same time that she plastered a bright smile on her face. ''Gosh, I sure wish I could. But…''

''Another time,'' Jack said.

Subtle. But there was something completely endearing about a man who wanted alone time with the woman he loved.

''Yeah,'' she said. ''Hey, Jack? Anything yet on you-know-who?''

She almost felt guilty asking. The man had his hands full with a new computer business. She'd taken care of the paperwork for his purchase of It's Geek To Me. He handled equipment and set up systems for large companies.

He shook his head. ''Nothing that will help. One of the problems tracking him is he doesn't seem to stay with one job very long. But so far he looks like a model citizen. I'm waiting for something to turn up on those prints. If it does, I'll let Grady know.''

''Okay,'' she said. ''Have a nice dinner, you two.''

''Count on it,'' he said, grabbing Maggie's hand as he sent her a look so full of love it was almost painful.

The door closed and she was alone. As she straightened the files on her desk, she put the one marked ''Adams vs. O'Connor'' on top. Her stomach clenched. There couldn't possibly be much time left. Four weeks was even more time than she'd hoped for. But—

As if the fates could read her mind, she glanced out her window and saw Hannah Morgan crossing

Main Street. Dev Hart was with her, holding her hand. Jen knew that Hannah had turned down a lucrative offer from a Los Angeles pediatric practice to stay in Destiny with Dev, the man she'd loved since high school.

Hannah opened the office door. "Hi, Jen."

"Hannah. Dev," she said to the tall man standing behind the diminutive blond doctor.

"Hey, Jen." Dev kept his hands protectively, possessively on Hannah's shoulders.

Hannah reached up and intertwined her fingers with his. "You look like you're closing up shop. Got a minute?"

"Sure."

"I got a call from his lawyer wondering about the DNA tests."

Jen didn't need to ask who she meant. Billy Bob Adams and what he was trying to do were never far from her thoughts. "And?"

"I couldn't delay," Hannah said. "I had to put a rush on it. According to the lab, the results should be back in a week."

"Okay. That's good to know."

Dev glanced down at his fiancée, then back at her. "Anything I can do to help Grady's case, all you have to do is say the word."

"Thanks. I'm working on Plan B."

"Good." He met her gaze. "Hannah and I are going to grab some dinner. Want to join us?"

"That's a great idea," Hannah agreed. "We're planning our wedding and I'd love some input. Mom is helping, but she's distracted. I don't know if you heard, but she and Frank, Doc Holloway, are planning to get married, too."

"I heard," Jen said. Loneliness welled up inside her threatening to swallow her whole. She drew on some soul-deep reserves of strength and managed a smile. "There's an epidemic of marriage mania sweeping Destiny. If it's something in the water, I'm going to start drinking bottled."

The happy couple standing just inside the doorway laughed. Dev slid his arms around Hannah's waist and pulled her back against him. "So join us. We'll buy you a bottle of something."

"I wish I could. But I've got plans."

Now, there was an out-and-out lie. But she was tired. She'd used up all her reserves on the happy smile a few moments ago. What she needed was a long soak in the tub. A romance novel, because her reserves on that were pretty low, too. And bed. Alone.

How pathetic was that?

"Maybe next time," Dev said. Though the invitation had been his idea, clearly he was not disappointed he would be spending the evening alone with the woman he loved. "Have a good evening."

Then they were gone. She turned her back on that damn window. It had seemed like a good idea when she was looking for office space. But if one more disgustingly happy couple walked through her door, she was afraid she would scream. Or worse. Burst into tears.

She straightened the files on her desk, then grabbed her purse. Behind her the door opened. Bracing herself, she turned around. Fortunately it wasn't another happy couple. Unfortunately it was one very available, very hunky-looking Grady O'Connor. Just the man she wanted to see, and not see.

"Hi," she said.

"Hi, yourself." He shut the door and came into the room, standing right in front of her. "You look tired."

You look good enough to kiss, she thought. For one heart-stopping moment she thought she'd said the words out loud. When his expression didn't change, she figured she was safe.

"I'm a little tired," she admitted.

She realized the two of them hadn't exchanged any meaningful conversation since that day at Hannah's office, when the girls had suggested their own Plan B—marrying their father. Jen's heart pounded at the thought.

Grady stepped closer and touched one finger to her chin, nudging it up so he could study her face. "You've got bags under your eyes big enough to pack for an extended trip to Europe."

Apparently looking good enough to kiss was one-sided. "How often has that silver tongue of yours landed you in a heap of trouble, hotshot?"

He grinned. "Would you believe never?"

"No."

"Seriously, Jen. You look like you've been burning the candle at both ends."

He surveyed her from the top of her head, down to her silky white blouse tucked into her straight navy skirt, the panty hose covering her legs and into her sensible low-heeled matching navy pumps. This is what the well-dressed attorney wore on a day she met with a prospective lucrative client.

"I've been busy. Trying to drum up business for the firm."

"I haven't seen much of you."

"Yeah. No news is good news." She sighed. "Especially considering the news I've got."

"What?"

"Hannah said the DNA results will be back in about a week. That means we'll be in court. I just talked to Jack and he's going to step up his efforts." She shrugged. "Pretty soon it's show time."

He nodded, the lines beside his nose and mouth deepening. "Okay."

"If there's nothing else, I'll say good-night."

"Actually, there is something." He folded his arms over his chest. "Have dinner with me."

Invitation number three. Third time's the charm. Then common sense prevailed. Spending time with him could be hazardous to her heart. It didn't matter that thoughts of him were never far from her mind. That was bad enough. But putting herself smack-dab in his presence, with the sight of him so handsome he took her breath away. The deep tones of his voice raising tingles on her body from head to toe. His masculine scent that surrounded her, practically seducing her. She already knew how good he tasted, thanks to kissing him twice. If he touched her one more time she could be a goner in a big way.

"Don't you have to get home to the twins?"

He shook his head. "They're at a sleepover. The house is going to be pretty quiet."

Great. She was a delaying tactic to keep from going home to an empty house. Then she realized it had to have crossed his mind that the house could be empty permanently if he lost custody. Nothing like feeling the pressure during her work day and after hours, too.

"Grady, I don't think I have the energy to have dinner with you."

Frown lines deepened in his forehead. "I didn't realize it took energy."

''Bad phrasing. I wouldn't be very good company.''

''Me, either. We can be bad company together. Who else would put up with us?''

The corners of her mouth curved up. Damn him. How did he do that? Make her smile, especially when he had his own problems. How was she supposed to resist him?

''I don't know…''

''Look, Jen, we've already established you're tired. If you were one of my deputies, I'd send you home with orders not to come back to work for a week.''

''That's not possible. And lucky for you I'm not one of your deputies.''

But how sweet was that? He was concerned about her. But that wasn't possible. Worry implied caring a lot. He was just her friend and also the sheriff showing professional concern for a citizen.

''You need to get your mind off my case for a while. Sometimes when you think too hard about something, it pushes the answers further out of reach.''

She lifted one eyebrow. ''This is a switch. Usually it's the attorney who takes the client out to dinner.''

''Okay, Counselor. We can do it your way. How about this? We need to have a council of war to discuss strategy for the court battle.''

He was apparently quite a dedicated sheriff determined to look out for her. It was the one argument she couldn't ignore.

She wagged her finger at him. ''Smooth, Sheriff. An invitation like that is impossible for a girl like me to resist.''

Grady stared across the shined-to-a-see-your-face-in-it gloss top of a picnic table at a restaurant two towns over from Destiny. It was dark, not fancy, but the food was great. He'd sold Jen with the "best barbecue in Texas" line, especially since she'd said she didn't want to run into anyone they knew. Sitting there in her city-slicker, sophisticated lawyer suit, she looked as out of place as a princess at a rodeo. But the way she was putting away the all-you-can-eat ribs gave him hope.

As well as kicking up his lust factor. It was impossible to eat ribs and stay pristine. She had sauce on her mouth, her fingers and a splatter on the breast of her silky white blouse. He wanted to kiss it off—everywhere. Yeah, that would happen. Maybe in an alternative universe. Or with someone other than Jensen Stevens. And that was the trouble. He hadn't met anyone he wanted more than her.

If he was going to make it through the evening without embarrassing himself, he needed to take his mind off stuff like that—more specifically, her mouth.

"So tell me—why did you want to go some place where we wouldn't run into anyone from Destiny?" he asked, remembering her directive when he'd inquired about her dinner location preferences.

Still holding a rib in both hands, she looked up. "What makes you think I had a reason?"

"Come on, Jen. This is me." And you're you, he thought.

"Okay, I'll come clean."

"All evidence to the contrary," he said wryly.

She grinned as she put down the rib then ripped open the packet containing a wet wipe and cleaned her face and hands.

"I haven't had ribs that good in ages," she admitted.

"Yeah, I bet Dallas doesn't do anything so unsophisticated."

Was he trying to tip the scales in his favor? She'd set up a branch office for her firm in Destiny. That didn't mean she would stay permanently to run it. Why would she stay in a town with nothing but bad memories?

"Dallas might surprise you," was all she said. "As far as why I wanted to go to a place far from Destiny—I was getting weird vibes."

He blinked. "You're going to have to explain that one."

"Okay." She pushed her plate away, then took a sip of her white wine. "Just before you walked into my office I had separate visits from Maggie and Jack, then Hannah and Dev. They were all going out to dinner."

"I still don't get it."

"They're couples now."

"So?"

"Aside from the fact that they're so in love I have to bite my tongue to keep from saying get a room, it gives me a weird feeling. They were involved in some way ten years ago. It's déjà vu all over again."

"Yeah. I know what you mean. I felt the ripples when Mitch came back to town. Seems like it's about time things settled."

"Ten years." She sighed, a big, gusty sound. "A decade. When you think about what happened ten years ago…" She looked up at him. "I meant with Taylor and Mitch. Hannah and Dev. Jack and Maggie. They're all getting married. It's as if the world is finally righting itself."

"You're certainly waxing nostalgic tonight."

"I never wax anything if I can possibly avoid it," she said, laughing. "But three couples have recently become engaged and I've had visits tonight from two of them."

"Maybe you and I will be next," he said. Where the hell had that come from?

"Don't you start," she warned.

Start? He hadn't just started. In fact, he knew exactly where that had come from. Something had become painfully clear. The want hadn't just begun. He'd always wanted Jen. Even ten years ago. But no way could he have acted on it then. With the death of his parents in that car accident, his life had turned upside down. So he'd wanted her from afar. And watched her go out with Mitch. Then Zach had moved in on her and the rest was history.

Instead of responding to her words, he said, "Are you aware that every guy who went to Destiny High School had the hots for you?"

Her eyes widened, then she laughed. "Way to go, Sheriff. You said I needed to forget about the custody case for a while and that did it."

"I'm dead serious. Every single heterosexual guy older or younger—age was inconsequential when it came to worshiping at your feet—every last one wanted *you*."

She blinked, then stared at him for several moments. "Including you?" Her voice was a husky whisper.

"You bet. I was their leader."

"But I don't…" She stopped and shook her head.

"Do you ever wonder what would have happened if you'd taken another road ten years ago?" he asked.

She laughed without humor. "That's a diplomatic way of putting it. Of course I wonder. With me out of the equation, Zach would have been single and in a position to do the right thing by Lacey. He would have married her and taken responsibility for the girls.''

''Not necessarily…''

''Of course. What was I thinking?'' she asked, shrugging. ''That crush thing was just a joke. You would have married Lacey no matter what. You love her.''

He wondered about her use of present tense. Did she think he was still in love with Lacey? She'd indicated more than once that she thought he'd loved his wife very much, because he'd married her and raised another man's children. It was time to come clean about the past, to set the record straight—to set things *right*. All of it.

''Jen?'' He met her gaze, willing her to listen and believe what he was going to say. ''About Lacey and me. I never loved her. Not the way you're thinking. Not as more than a friend.''

Chapter Ten

Jen held her breath. He'd had a crush on her ten years ago? He never loved Lacey? Any second an alien spacecraft would appear and beam her up. The world was spinning out of control—that's all it would take to finish her off.

"I don't believe you," she said, standing. "It's a lie. Why would you say something like that?"

But the serious, open, honest look on his handsome face scared her. Waiting to hear more wasn't an option. She whirled around and walked away from him. Heading for the exit, she saw a sign for the rest room. Good idea. She felt grimy, and not just from eating ribs. A decade of dirt weighed her down. She went in, then stopped in front of the sink. After turning on the water, she washed her hands, then splashed the coolness in her face. Good Lord. Was everything about the past ten years a lie?

Grady had had a crush on her? She looked in the mirror, at her haunted eyes with bags large enough to pack for an extended trip to Europe. He was right. She looked awful. Probably because she felt awful. Surely any attraction he'd felt had flickered out after she'd run off with Zach.

Sighing, she realized she couldn't stay in the bathroom forever, no matter how much she might want to. And she wanted to a lot. More than anything she wished she could be by herself. But they'd dropped her car off at Taylor's ranch. Grady had driven the two of them to dinner. Right about now he probably thought she'd lost her mind, and was calling the sheriff's department dispatch to send out the men in the white coats. So maybe she didn't need a ride home after all.

When she left the ladies' room, the impossibly young, blond, blue-eyed hostess stopped her. "The man you came in with said to tell you he's waiting for you by the car."

Jen nodded. "Thanks."

She walked outside and a warm breeze cooled her still-damp cheeks. Only the lights from the restaurant kept the parking lot from pitch-blackness. Beyond the nuisance light, stars twinkled in the inky-black Texas sky. Any other time, under different circumstances, she would appreciate this beautiful night. It would take a heart of stone not to notice that romance swirled in the air. She *so* didn't want romance.

Taking a deep breath, she spotted Grady. In the first parking space by the door, he leaned against the passenger side of his black sport utility vehicle. All she could see was his back, and she wondered what he was thinking. He'd changed out of his uniform at the office. His broad shoulders looked even wider in the white cotton shirt. The vehicle blocked her view of the rest of him. And that was a damn shame considering he had one spectacular butt—in uniform or jeans. Still, burned into her memory was an image of the soft denim molded to his lean hips and muscular thighs.

Good grief, she was an idiot. Standing there drooling was completely counterproductive. Unless she was prepared to hoof it home, she had to actually *see* him again. Knowing that if he wasn't telling a whopper, ten years ago he'd had a crush on her.

He glanced at her when her shoes clicked on the blacktop. She walked around the front of the car and stood in front of him.

"I wouldn't lie to you, Jen."

Somehow she'd known. His words had shocked her, but she would bet her life that Grady O'Connor didn't lie. Which meant he'd definitely noticed her in high school. But she couldn't think about that now. Let alone talk about it.

"Why did you marry her? I know you told me she was running away because she was afraid. But she had nothing to be ashamed of. There were other ways you could have helped."

"If anyone should understand it's you. We were young." He folded his arms over his chest. "She was desperate. It seemed like the right thing to do. She was afraid her dad would do something to Zach. Get himself into trouble. If he'd found out…"

"I wish he had. If the truth had come out then, maybe—"

"What? You wouldn't have married Zach?"

"Maybe. Yes. No. I don't know." Damn, she was confused. "Zach should have done the right thing. If not voluntarily, then by force."

"The timing was off."

"Because he was already married," she clarified, guilt knotting her insides.

"Yeah. Lacey didn't see any way out but to run."

"That still doesn't explain why you married her. When you didn't love her," she added.

"I owed her family. They were there for me after my folks were killed in the accident. I had less than a year till graduation. But I was already eighteen and ineligible for state assistance. The Millers took me in because Lacey insisted. She and I were best friends, and with their help I could finish high school."

"But she was pregnant with another man's child," she protested.

"It was her child, too."

"A child you'd be responsible for."

He shrugged. "She was desperate. Marriage solved her immediate problem. I could do that."

Jen remembered what he'd told her before—that Lacey lived long enough for Grady and her father to reconcile. "It created some problems, too. Her father thought you got her pregnant, didn't he?"

Grady took off his hat and ran his hands through his hair. He set the Stetson on the hood of the car, then glanced at her. "Yeah. He accused me of using their hospitality and generosity to get what I wanted."

"Even if that was true, you did the right thing. You married her," Jen protested. "Why was he so angry that it took months to settle things between you?"

Even in the dim light from the restaurant, she could see the bleak expression in his eyes. "I didn't understand then, but I do now. It's all about a father's unconditional love. He was furious at me, assuming I'd taken advantage of his little girl. God knows if I were in his shoes, and some guy married one of my girls under the circumstances he thought, I'd probably react the same way. And I can understand why Lacey was afraid he would do something to get himself into trouble.''

''She was responsible for the two of you burying the hatchet?''

He nodded. ''She insisted. She knew she was dying. But she wouldn't let go until she made the two of us promise to raise the babies together. And we did.''

''He never knew the girls weren't yours?''

''They *are* mine,'' he said fiercely. ''Lacey gave them to me.''

''I'm sorry. Bad choice of words. He never knew the truth?''

Grady shook his head. ''And he never knew I didn't love her—not as more than a friend. Not the way she deserved to be loved. And until the day he died, I kept from him the truth about the night they were conceived.''

Jen moved beside him. She wanted to take him in her arms, but she was afraid. So she leaned against the car's front fender, so close to Grady that her hip brushed against his thigh. She wasn't sure what to do with the information he'd just revealed. Emotionally speaking, she had a bad feeling she was in deep trouble. But she couldn't go there. She turned her thoughts to his custody case. And what Billy Bob's lawyer had said in court. Grady had custody of the girls and a ranch that wasn't his.

''So when Lacey's dad died, he left the ranch to you?''

''Yeah. He said I was the son he'd never had and the father of his granddaughters. It ate at me—keeping the secret. But he was dying and there was no peace for him in telling the truth then.''

''Billy Bob's lawyers could make a case that you kept it to yourself to get your hands on the money that rightfully belongs to the girls.''

''And they'd be wrong,'' he said, his voice full of passionate intensity. ''Clark Livingston handled the will. I had him put everything into trust for the girls. I only manage the ranch. Any profits pay the bills and get channeled back into the operation.''

''Why did you tell me all this, Grady?''

He looked down at her, but his eyes gave nothing away. ''I figured it was about time to take myself off the pedestal you had me on. Besides, you need to have all the facts. We don't want any surprises to come out in the courtroom. The fact is I'm a selfish so-and-so.''

''How can you say that?'' she cried. ''You've raised those girls without getting anything in return.''

''That's where you're wrong.'' He folded his arms over his chest. ''I did what I thought was right. I owed the Millers and it was an easy way for me to pay them back. But the fact is, I got everything in return. Those two girls are my whole world. I can't give them up. Maybe that's selfish. It's not for me to judge. But, by God, I'll do my damnedest to give them something back. When Kasey and Stacey are of age, I intend to turn over one of the most prosperous ranches in Destiny.''

''Well, then, we have to do everything we can to see that your intentions are realized,'' she said.

He let out a long breath. ''I'm glad you see things my way, Counselor.''

''I do.'' When she glanced at him, she saw a flash of white teeth in the dim light. ''What?''

"I do. Two little words that give a man ideas."

"What kind of ideas?" she asked, narrowing her gaze.

"Ideas like—why don't you marry me?"

"What?"

"I think the girls were onto something."

"Don't you remember? I explained to them two people get married because they love each other. It's the first, best and only reason to take the long walk down the aisle." She stopped and shook her head. "But look who I'm talking to. The man who marries damsels in distress." She frowned. "Not that I'm in distress. You get my drift."

"What if we fall in love?" he asked.

"We won't. We can't." She sidled away from him. "That's impossible."

"Why? I've already confessed my crush. And you didn't deny that whole pedestal thing I had going on."

How could she? He'd been right on the money. She had a serious case of hero worship. And he'd confessed his deep, dark secret, then said he was selfish. Ha! If everyone in the world were so self-centered the human race would be living in Mr. Rogers's neighborhood. She was afraid, very afraid. She didn't want to care about a man again. Especially a man who had good reason to not care about her in return.

"This discussion is pointless," she said, moving away from him.

"You told the girls that if I was married my chances in court improved."

"Your chances *might* improve if you married anyone but me."

"Why do I think this isn't about legal ramifications at all?"

"Because it isn't. And I think you should take me home now."

She opened the passenger door and started to step up. It was high. In her short, straight, tight skirt, there was no way she could get in and leave her dignity intact. She turned around, and he was right there in front of her. His chest wide, strong, stable. Comforting. Yet he made her *uncomfortable* at the same time. In a sensuous way.

"What are you afraid of, Jen?"

"I'm afraid to climb in and flash you with the promised land."

One corner of his mouth curved up. "That's not what I meant, and you know it."

"Since you don't seem inclined to let this drop, think about it, Grady. How ironic is it that you married without love because Lacey was pregnant. You fell in love with the twins. To keep them, your best chance is to marry—again without love."

"What if we fall in love?" he asked for the second time, his voice husky, deep, seductive.

"First of all, it can't happen because I won't let it. This case is too important. I can't afford the distraction. You know that."

"Horse manure. What's second of all?"

"Huh?"

"You said first of all. That implies there's more. Lay it on me."

"Second of all, think about it. What chance could we possibly have?"

"A better one than most people."

"Most guys wouldn't give a tumble to the widow of the jerk who did what Zach did to Lacey. Whether you loved her romantically or not doesn't matter. You were her friend and cared enough to help her out of a jam. A jam my husband was responsible for. It's too big a hurdle.''

He reached out and put his hands at her waist, and in one smooth, effortless movement lifted her onto the vehicle seat. No promised-land peekaboo. Always the nice guy. Once a hero, always a hero.

''You're wrong,'' he said softly, hardly more than a deep whisper.

Since his hands were still at her waist, warm and welcoming, and chipping away at her resolve, she rested *her* hands on his shoulders. ''And what about the girls?''

''What about them? They think you're the best thing since Dude Ranch Barbie.''

She couldn't help smiling at that. ''As flattering as that is, I don't deserve it.''

''Why not? Granted, you're not as tall, proportionately speaking. Or as well endowed. But that's highly overrated. I'm here to tell you that a man doesn't care about that sort of thing. All we want is to see our woman naked—''

''Stop!''

''What?''

''You're deliberately muddying the waters.'' Mother Nature had just cranked up the outside temperature. That had to be the reason she was hot all over. ''Okay. For the sake of argument. What if we fall in love? How could you ever trust my judgment, Grady?''

His gaze smoldered. There was no other word to describe the expression. ''When are you going to stop being afraid and take a chance?''

''I don't know…''

"Yes, you do."

He leaned forward and touched his lips to hers. She could muster only a split second of resistance before giving herself up to the sensation. Coming home. That's how he made her feel. She sighed against his mouth, then opened her own to him. Hungrily. He swept his tongue inside, and the contact sensitized every nerve in her body. Her skin was hot and any second she could go up in flames. When he slid her closer, she almost expected to see a shower of sparks. Instead, her skirt rode up to her hips and she opened her knees, permitting him between them.

Her breath hiked up along with her skirt. The only thing separating them, as far as flesh to flesh was concerned, was her panty hose and his jeans. Liquid heat flowed through her, making her insides as hot as her skin. He pressed her to him—soft breasts to muscled chest. She could feel his heart racing, and her own kept pace. She wrapped her arms around his neck, kissing him with everything she had. It wasn't smart. In fact, it was probably the dumbest thing she'd ever done. But she was beyond caring.

All she wanted was to be in this man's arms forever. If he never stopped kissing her, holding her, she would be the happiest woman in the world. She would give him everything.

She dragged her mouth from his and nibbled along his strong jaw, ignoring the scrape of five-o'clock shadow against her lips. When she ran her tongue around his earlobe, she heard him hiss out a breath. She smiled, ecstatic that she wasn't the only one feeling the earth move. She was putty in his hands and couldn't find the will to care.

She kissed his neck. "Grady, we need..."

Breathing hard, he pulled back. "I trust you implicitly. When are you going to let yourself trust me?"

"I do."

He shook his head. "No, you don't. But you can. The reason I know is because I'm this close to the promised land, but I'm not crossing over. Not until you're ready to trust me not to hurt you."

"I'm ready," she protested. "Believe me."

"But you'd have regrets," he said, dragging in air. "I'll wait. And you can take this to the bank—waiting is not easy. Damn, it's the hardest thing I've ever done." He removed her hands from around his neck and kissed her right palm, then folded her fingers in on it. "It's time to set the past to rights. I'm not about to make another mistake."

Dazed, she blinked at him. "But..."

"No buts. *Now* I'll take you home."

He backed away, gently pressed her knees together, swung her legs around, then slammed the car door. Along with her slender hopes. She couldn't believe it. She'd kissed Grady O'Connor with complete abandon.

At least one of them had kept a cool head. Sure as heck wasn't her. She should be grateful to him for giving her a dash of reality and a cold reminder. All his talk about trusting him was to let her down easily. Always the hero. If he cared the way she did, he wouldn't be able to turn his back on what she'd offered. But the truth was he'd saved her from making a big mistake.

Her belief in happily ever after had died with Zach. *Nothing* that had happened since had changed her mind.

Not even tonight. Although she was very much

afraid the shattering sound she heard was her heart breaking.

Five days after his dinner with Jen, Grady sat behind his desk trying to work. He needed to get through a stack of paperwork big enough to choke a horse. But every time he tried, he saw Jen's face. The fear in her eyes when she'd said, "What if we fall in love?"

There was no "what if" about it. Not for him. Not anymore.

His intercom buzzed and he pushed the button. "Yeah?"

"Whoa." Phoebe's voice was rife with questions. "Who tweaked your tail? You said no calls and you weren't seeing anyone short of the president of the United States. I swear no one got past me, Sheriff."

"What is it, Deputy?"

"Jensen Stevens is here to see you."

A surge of adrenaline mushroomed inside him. He hadn't seen her in the flesh since that night. Since he'd kissed her to within an inch of his self-control. He'd begun to think she was avoiding him. Then he remembered how afraid she'd looked at the idea of loving him and *knew* she'd been avoiding him. The only reason she'd be here to see him was about the custody case.

"Sheriff? Grunt or something so I'll know you're still with me?"

"Funny, Phoebe."

"Thanks. I try."

"Send Miss Stevens in."

"*Miss?*"

"Don't go there, Phoebs."

"Yes, sir. I mean, no, sir," she snapped out just before clicking off.

A few moments later there was a knock on his door, then it opened. "Can I come in?"

He stood up. "Yeah. Have a seat," he said, indicating the chairs in front of his desk.

She was a sight for sore eyes. In her green sundress she looked like a walking meadow and smelled just as sweet.

"This won't take that long. Hannah Morgan called me," she said, still standing. "The DNA results are in."

He ran a hand through his hair. "And?"

"She said there are no surprises. There's over a ninety-five-percent certainty that Zach is their biological father."

"Okay."

"Billy shows a family connection. Which we also knew."

"Right."

She took a deep breath. "There's no possible way, genetically, that you could be their father."

"So it's exactly what we expected."

"Yeah. But that's not all." She met his gaze, uncertainty in her eyes. "We've got a date in Judge Kellerman's court for a week from today."

"Good," he said, sitting down. "The sooner the better."

"I've lined up character witnesses. I'll give you the list. Let me know if there's anyone missing. Anyone you can think of who will testify that you've got wings, a halo and can walk on water."

"That leaves out my staff," he joked. "And probably anyone I've arrested."

Her mouth curved up, reminding him how sweet her lips had tasted that night under the stars. But the serious look on her face told him she wouldn't appreciate him sharing the thought. Geez. Enough. He had to concentrate. He couldn't do that when he was preoccupied with thoughts of kissing his legal representation.

"I'm sure there are a lot of people in town who would be more than happy to stipulate as to your good name. And your positive effect on the girls. Like they said, everyone in Destiny loves their dad. I'll make sure you get a copy of the list."

"Okay." He glanced at the photo of his twins smiling at him from the frame on his desk. He loved those girls more than anything. Only them, until now. He looked at Jensen and suddenly he couldn't breathe. He had to find a way to convince her of how he felt.

She gripped the back of the visitor's chair so hard her knuckles turned white. "I have the report that the department of social services compiled from their home evaluation."

"What good will that do?"

"I'm sure Billy's lawyers did the same. Since he's living in a rundown motel outside of town..."

"I don't see how that will help, since he's planning to move to the ranch when—*if*—he gets custody."

"The judge won't miss the contrast, Grady. She can't. You've spent the last nine years doing a great job of raising these girls. If he can't provide a good home on his own, she's going to have to make the connection that he's a money-grubbing bottom feeder."

"Is that the correct legal definition?"

"You *bet* it is," she said.

His humor faded. He didn't believe it would happen. But Jen had warned him about the unpredictability of the situation. He had to be realistic. "What if it's not enough to cancel out his biological link? After all, he is their uncle. Now we have the proof."

Her expression was grim. "Thanks to me."

"I didn't say that."

"You didn't have to. I've thought it enough for both of us. I think I'll go see Jack."

"No. Let me." He stood up.

"Okay. His new store must have state-of-the-art technology." She walked over to the doorway, then turned back. "In the meantime, I've got a week to come up with a brilliant strategy. Ten ways to beat a bottom feeder at his own game."

Grady sensed that everything in his world was riding on this case. He felt Jen's intensity to win and wondered why. He had no hard evidence, but his gut told him if she lost in court, any chance they might have had together would be lost, too.

Chapter Eleven

Someone shook her shoulder. Jensen sat up, disoriented, heart hammering. She glanced around through sleep-blurred eyes. One look out the window told her it was dark. Where was she?

"Jen? It's Grady."

"Oh, gosh," she said, blinking up at him. Then she took another look around. This was her office, her desk. "I guess I fell asleep. What time is it?"

"Way past time for you to go home."

She looked at her watch. "Holy moley. Eleven o'clock."

"Yeah." Without bothering to take himself around to the visitor side, he leaned a hip against the corner of her desk. The corner that was right inside her personal work space.

Her heart rate, just slowing from the abrupt awakening, kicked up again. Then she remembered why she'd been working late. Tomorrow she had to go into court armed with a rock and a slingshot and convince Goliath he wasn't untouchable after all.

The problem was a rock and a slingshot didn't seem to be enough when the opposition had biology going for them and the welfare of two little girls was at stake.

She met the sheriff's gaze. ''Tell me Jack has come up with something on Billy Bob Adams. I don't care if it's spitting on the sidewalk in Kalamazoo. All we have to do is show he's not the kind of person who should have custody of a pet rock, let alone children.''

Grady's expression was unreadable. He had his cop face on, not a good sign. ''Jack checked every law enforcement database from FBI to CIA. And some he couldn't even tell me about.''

''He ran the fingerprints?

''Yeah.''

''And?'' she asked hopefully.

''And…'' He shrugged.

''Damn. I'd bet everything I own the man is an opportunist who doesn't give a rat's backside whether that opportunity is on the right or wrong side of the law. I can't believe there's nothing to pin on him.''

''Yeah.''

She sighed, then rested her forearms on her desk and put her head on them. For so many reasons she wanted to win this case. First and foremost, the kids. Then there was the whole moral issue of making the past as right as it could be. How could she ever look Grady in the eye again if things went badly? This was probably why it wasn't a good idea to become emotionally involved with a client.

She'd tried so hard to resist him.

She'd hardly finished thinking that thought when strong arms slid beneath her knees and across her back. She was lifted out of her chair and snuggled against Grady's solid chest. Then he sat down in her very own chair with her on his very own lap.

Resisting him would be a lot easier if he would cooperate by not touching her and being too sweet for words.

"What are you doing?" she asked.

"At the risk of stating the obvious, I'm sitting in your chair."

"And why would you be doing that?" she asked, nestling just a little closer.

"Because I'm tired, too." He sighed.

She couldn't help it. She gave in to the overwhelming urge to rest her head on his shoulder and thanked the good Lord she'd had the excellent sense to purchase a really big chair.

"You should go home and get some rest," she suggested, although every part of her cried out against it.

She didn't want to be alone. No. It wasn't that. She'd been by herself for a long time now and had made peace with loneliness. It all had to do with wanting to be with Grady.

"That's the pot calling the kettle black. When do *you* plan to quit burning the midnight oil?" His voice dripped with irony and amusement.

"It's not midnight," she scoffed.

"You're splitting hairs."

"That's what a good attorney does." She'd always thought she was good. Until this case. Or was it just that there was so much riding on the verdict in this one?

"In another hour it will be midnight, and I'm running you out of town before that."

"Says who?"

"I'm the sheriff. Running people out of town is what I do." But instead of letting her go, he tightened his hold and the large, strong hand at her waist squeezed reassuringly. "Jen, you need to go home and get some rest. Things have a way of working out."

"But, Grady…"

He touched a finger to her lips. "In all those years of school, didn't anyone ever tell you there's a time to study? Then there's a time to put away the books and rest. Everything you need is right up here," he said, tapping his index finger gently against her temple. "You just need distance to see it."

She sighed. "I could hike all the way to San Antonio and still not see a way out of this."

"Okay. So tell me. What can we expect in court tomorrow?"

"The judge should have read all the briefs and depositions detailing why Kasey and Stacey should stay with you. I've cited your character and the fact that you're the sheriff. You've had custody of the girls since birth. They've never known another caregiver and always believed you to be their father."

"Do you think the fact that I didn't tell them the truth until recently will hurt my chances?"

"I thought of that. The issue is addressed in the brief. Everything from the way they were conceived to fulfilling their dying mother's wish by keeping it from their grandfather. After his death the most important thing was the twins' emotional stability. You provided that without a hitch."

"You make me sound good."

"An understatement." She smiled, tilting her head back to meet his gaze. "It was the easiest brief I ever prepared."

Because he was a good man. Making him sound like a knight in shining armor had been a piece of cake.

"What else did you say about me?" One eyebrow lifted in a self-satisfied expression.

"I'm finished feeding your inflated ego, Sheriff. I pointed out to the judge that it would be traumatic and disruptive to the girls' emotional development to be yanked out of the nurturing environment you've provided for them since birth."

"Anything else?"

"I took depositions from their teachers, principal, counselors and director at the summer camp where they're in day care. I've been all over Destiny interviewing anyone and everyone. If there's someone out there with a grudge against you, I couldn't track them down."

"No wonder you're tired." He snuggled her closer. "So why are you worried?"

"The damn DNA evidence. The court has an annoying habit of linking parental rights to biology. I don't know how heavily that family link will weigh with the judge."

"If there are outstanding warrants for his arrest, not very much," he pointed out.

"Who said he's a fugitive from the law?"

"No one."

She lifted her head to look at him. His voice sounded funny and lacked conviction. Because she was so close to him, she could feel something like expectation humming through him. She thought that was odd, but chalked it up to the fact that he had to be even more worried than she was.

She rested her cheek against his shoulder again.

"Since we couldn't find anything showing he's not fit, I'm going to hammer home the fact that he hasn't made an effort to contact them. Ever. Even if I can't convince the judge his goal is to get his hands on easy money, she'll have to see he doesn't care about the kids."

"I'm sure she will."

"I need to get him to tell the truth. He's so cold and calculating. Step by step I have to lead him into saying he doesn't really want the girls."

"It's going to be fine, Jen. You have to trust."

Trust? An emotional response. Then there was a trust—set up to safeguard financial holdings. Grady had told her he'd put everything in trust for the twins and he was the executor. She sat up, out of the circle of his arms.

"What?" he asked. "You've got a look on your face like you're locked and loaded and ready to kick some major butt."

"I've got an idea." She met his gaze. "It's risky, but it just might do the trick."

"I trust you."

There was that word again.

"Do you want to hear my idea?"

"If you want to tell me."

She frowned. Since when was he so indifferent? Or did he really believe in her that much? He was a good man, but was he that good? Could he actually have so much faith in her?

"You're my client. You have the most to gain—or lose. I'd like your take on this."

"Okay." But he tried to tug her back against his chest.

Heat coursed through her and she stood up. It was

hard to think about torts and depositions and briefs of the legal kind when he was so close that she could feel the warmth of his body and smell the scent of his skin. When she was wishing with every fiber of her being he would kiss her senseless.

She went around her desk and sat in one of the visitor chairs. "I need to get him to admit he doesn't really want the girls. That it's about the money he can get from the ranch."

"Right."

"The one you have in trust for them. The trust that you handle."

"What are you getting at?"

"What if I propose a compromise arrangement? He gets physical custody. You maintain your position as executor of the trust."

His eyes narrowed and the long, lean lines of his body tensed. "Why would he agree to that?"

"He wouldn't. I'm guessing it will catch him off guard and maybe he'll let something slip. Like he'd rather eat glass than be responsible for two nine-year-old girls."

Grady nodded and the tension disappeared. "Sounds good to me."

"That's all you have to say?"

He shrugged. "You're the lawyer. If you think it's our best shot, count me in."

"I think it could backfire and blow up in our face."

"That's not going to happen," he reassured her.

"How can you know that?" she asked.

"Because I know *you*."

The intensity in his eyes took her breath away and cranked up her heart rate by a lot. He stood and came around the desk and sat in the chair beside hers. Taking her hands in his, he said, "Remember what I said about needing distance to figure out what you know?"

She nodded. "Yeah. Have you ever needed distance—about anything?"

"Sure."

"Want to tell me what?"

"Yeah. You."

"I don't understand."

"Ten years ago I had a crush on you, but Zach was the guy you picked. I figured you were self-absorbed, like him. It took time and distance to show me I was wrong. You're so much more than I ever knew." He squeezed her hands. "You're going to grind Billy Bob Adams into the dust tomorrow."

"Grady, listen to me. This is a long shot. If Billy doesn't take the bait and the judge thinks it's a good idea, he'll get the girls."

"That's not going to happen."

"If it does, you'll never forgive me."

"If you're wrong, you'll never forgive yourself. And I'm not talking about this custody thing. You married the wrong man. That's all. You were young. You had no idea what he was capable of. It's in the past. You have to let it go. The girls are my problem. But you've taken them on. I appreciate everything you've done. More than I can say."

Tears filled her eyes and she tried to tell herself she was just tired. But that was so not the truth.

She was in love with Grady O'Connor.

Of all the lamebrained, stupid things to do, she'd gone and fallen for a client. And, as always, her timing for this realization couldn't have been worse. Why now? Tomorrow, he was facing losing his children. To keep it from happening, he'd placed all his faith in her—the woman who'd had the bad judgment to run away with Zach Adams. Grady O'Connor was either as dumb as she was or the bravest, most wonderful man she'd ever met.

And this was the worst possible time to discover he was the only man in the world who could make her happy. Because in less than twenty-four hours there was a very real possibility he would never speak to her again.

For so many years she'd mourned Zach, and he wasn't half the man Grady was. How in the world could he trust her with the future of his children?

"I have every faith in you, Jen," he said again, as if he could read her mind.

"That makes one of us," she said shakily. "But I promise you this, Grady. I will go into court tomorrow as prepared as I can possibly be. I will do the very best I can for you."

"There's not a doubt in my mind."

He leaned toward her and she was sure he was going to kiss her. And he did. A sweet, chaste kiss on the forehead. So much for passion.

But he had faith in her. That meant there was a chance. What if they fell in love? A classic case of jumping the gun. First she had to get through tomorrow.

Grady walked up the courthouse steps and spotted Jen by the door, several feet away. She had notes in her hand, and all her concentration was focused there. It gave him an opportunity to study her without hiding his absolute, unbridled, male appreciation.

The counselor had dressed to kill. Three-inch navy pumps made her legs look as if they went on forever—

not easy to do for a woman hardly bigger than a minute. Her pin-striped navy suit had a short skirt and fitted jacket that made her look trim, professional and guaranteed to make the town sheriff ready to rock and roll.

And how stupid was he? Letting feelings for her get to him. He should have seen this coming when he agreed to accept her legal counsel. His only excuse was he hadn't ever expected to fall for anyone. She'd zoomed in under his radar and now there would be hell to pay.

He wasn't sure what that hell was and couldn't think too far ahead. He sensed a lot was riding on this case and had finally figured out why. She needed to win—to make up for what she thought she'd done in the past. It had taken all his "cop face" skill to keep her from seeing his excitement last night. And he felt guilty for not sharing with her what Jack had found. But he'd had to chance it. For their future.

All he could do was give her this day in court. He walked closer and stood beside her, breathing in the scent of her perfume.

She glanced up, then did a double take. "Hi. I almost didn't recognize you. Not bad, Sheriff."

He'd worn a dark gray suit and red tie, just like the last time. He didn't want to give Billy Bob Adams any reason to be suspicious. It was touch and go, but he'd planned everything step by step. There was no reason to believe it wouldn't go off without a hitch.

"You don't look so bad yourself," he said. "If the judge was a man, you could convince him of anything."

"I'm going to believe that was meant as a sincere

compliment and not take you to task for the sexist
remark I heard.''

"Good. Because I meant it in the nicest possible
way.''

Her gaze narrowed. "How can you look so calm?
In a few minutes we'll find out if everything we've
worked for will convince a *female* judge to let you
retain custody of those children. You couldn't possibly
look more cool and collected.''

"Who says I'm cool?'' He smiled, hoping to disarm
her.

When this hearing was over, would she understand
what he'd done? More important—why he'd done it?

"Then you deserve an Academy Award.'' Eyes narrowed suspiciously, she met his gaze. "Clark Livingston isn't going to be here.''

"I know. He's officially retired, thanks to you.''

"Me?''

He nodded. "Now that there's a competent attorney
in town he's putting his shingle out to pasture.''

"Backup would have been nice,'' she muttered.

"Chin up, Counselor. Everything's going to be
fine.''

He hoped.

"It's now or never,'' she answered, letting out a
long breath.

"Right.'' He opened the door and she preceded him
into the building.

Side by side they walked down the aisle and
through the swinging doors to the tables set up in front
of the bench. Along with his attorney, who looked like
an ad from *GQ*, Billy Bob was there. When Jen
passed, the weasel glanced at her legs, and Grady
didn't like it one bit. The look in his eyes made

Grady's hands itch. He wanted to put them around the guy's neck and squeeze. Not an especially professional reaction. But he couldn't help it. He was only human. Particularly where Jensen Stevens was concerned. With an effort, he put on what she called his "cop face."

Before they could sit, the bailiff announced Judge Kellerman. She swept into the courtroom and sat behind the bench as the session came to order.

Judge Kellerman settled granny glasses on the end of her nose. "I've read all the material in the case and—"

Jen stood. "Your Honor, I have a proposal for the court's consideration."

"Is this something that wasn't in the brief?"

"Yes, Your Honor. But I think it will be a fair compromise in this case. The last thing Grady O'Connor wants is to deprive the children he loves from knowing their biological family."

That was a bald-faced lie, Grady thought. But he knew she was playing the game. He hoped she would understand why he had to do the same.

"Go on, Counselor." The judge took off her glasses and gave Jen her full attention.

"I propose to give Mr. Adams custody of the girls—Kasey and Stacey O'Connor." She paused dramatically.

Grady glanced at the worthless man across the aisle. He smirked, shooting back a self-satisfied expression. *Just wait, you low-life—*

"That's a surprise, Counselor," the judge was saying.

"Yes. But we think it's a fair and equitable solution.

The only thing we ask is that Sheriff O'Connor remain executor of the estate now in trust for the twins."

Grady glanced across the aisle again and nodded slightly at the shocked look on the other man's face. Not to mention the attorney's expression. The lawyer jumped to his feet. "Objection, Your Honor."

"You'll get your turn, Counselor. Let's hear Miss Stevens out."

Jen nodded her thanks. "Your Honor, the sheriff has taken excellent care of the girls' birthright. It's a thriving property. I've provided you with records showing that all profits have been funneled back into the operation of the ranch. Since he's doing such an outstanding job of protecting the assets, I submit there's no good reason to change the arrangement."

The judge nodded as she glanced through the papers in front of her. "Yes. It's all here."

"With that stipulation, Sheriff O'Connor withdraws his opposition to Mr. Adams's request for physical custody of the children."

Grady looked over and watched with growing satisfaction as Billy Bob conferred with his attorney. Jen had been cool and concise. Her argument was well thought out and beautifully delivered and she had the opposition scrambling. She'd been great. Every nerve ending in his body urged him to pull her into his arms and kiss her with all he had. And this was where his law enforcement training came in handy. He cautioned himself to patience. The trap hadn't been sprung yet.

At the opposing counsel's table voices rose in anger. Billy's face turned red. "What does that mean?"

The judge cleared her throat. "Let me explain it to you, Mr. Adams. You can have the children you claim to want, but you won't get your hands on their money.''

Billy stood and faced the bench. ''That's not fair. How am I gonna take care of them? Provide food, clothes, a roof over their heads?'' he protested.

''Get a job, Mr. Adams,'' Judge Kellerman said.

''But, that's not enough to pay for everything. I need the money.''

He kept talking, digging himself in deeper as his lawyer tried unsuccessfully to get him to sit down.

The judge yanked off her glasses and stared at him. ''Mr. Adams, Grady O'Connor has been a rancher and father at the same time he's worked for the sheriff's department for almost ten years now. I'm sure he'd be willing to talk you through it.''

Billy leaned over to listen to something his counsel was saying. ''It's not cheap raising kids these days. And I have to give those two kids my time. The money would help me out…''

''Well, you're not going to get it, Mr. Adams.'' Judge Kellerman shook her head slightly. ''I agree with Miss Stevens. It's a fair and equitable compromise. You can have the children, but Sheriff O'Connor will maintain his sound handling of their estate.''

Billy's benevolent-uncle expression disappeared. His eyes turned hard and his face contorted with rage as he met Grady's gaze. He glared at the judge as his hands clenched into fists. ''Forget it. I don't want those two brats. This is a rip-off and you're all in on it. I'm outta here.''

He walked through the swinging doors separating counsel tables from the spectator chairs. Grady turned to watch the show. Satisfaction eased through him as he saw Deputies Haines and Johnson blocking Billy's way. Jack was sitting there, too, a wide grin on his face as he nodded.

Phoebe tapped her uniform pocket. "Mr. Adams, I have a warrant for your arrest."

"What's going on, Grady?" Jen looked down at him, the same shock in her expression that laced her voice.

This was where he had to do some fast talking, he thought.

"You can't do this to me." Billy tried to get past the deputies, but Haines grabbed one arm and forcefully pulled it up behind his back, cuffing the wrist. He easily caught the other arm and subdued him to be Mirandized. "I haven't done anything," Billy protested.

"Yeah. And I'm the queen of England." Phoebe glared at the suspect. "You have the right to remain silent. If you give up that right, anything you say can and will be used against you in a court of law. If you can't afford an attorney—"

"He can't afford this one. Good luck." Billy's lawyer shot him a look of contempt and moved quickly by the three of them in the aisle. "You'll need it," he said, then walked out of the courtroom.

"An attorney will be provided," Phoebe finished. "Anything you want to add, Sheriff?"

A muscle jumped in Grady's jaw. He wanted to add a lot but all he said was, "Lock him up."

"With pleasure." She took the seething suspect's other arm.

Billy was mad as hell and sputtering incoherently. Grady had never taken more gratification from his job and a successful takedown as he did on this one. The deputies led the suspect from the court.

Judge Kellerman cleared her throat. "I suppose it's unnecessary to say this, Sheriff. I've known you for a long time. But you *do* have the proper paperwork on this arrest."

He stood up. "Yes, Your Honor. The charges are on file with the court."

"That's what I thought. And by the way, you get to keep your kids."

"Thanks, Your Honor."

"Don't mention it. I guess this hearing is adjourned," she said, then left the bench and disappeared through a door behind it.

Jen met his gaze as doubt and shadows swirled in her own. "What's going on, Grady?"

Before he could answer, Jack Riley joined them. "Way to go, Sheriff."

"I couldn't have done it without your help, Jack. Thanks," he said, holding out his hand.

"Glad I could help."

"I'd be glad, too, if someone would clue me in," Jen said.

Grady rubbed the back of his neck. "The short version is he's wanted in more than one state for some really bad stuff under a whole bunch of assumed names. Jack finally hit pay dirt."

"I didn't do much."

"You had the state-of-the-art equipment and the know-how to use it," Grady pointed out.

Jack shrugged modestly. "I wish I could hang around for the celebration with you two, but I'm meeting Maggie for lunch. We're making plans to get married."

"Congratulations, Jack." Grady held his hand out and the other man shook it.

"Thanks. I'll see you around."

"Later, buddy," Grady said, exhilaration coursing through him.

He felt like the luckiest guy in the world. Then he looked at Jen and the expression on her face told him his luck had just run out.

Chapter Twelve

Feeling an acute need for some fresh air, Jen followed Jack Riley from the courtroom without a word to Grady. How could she say anything? She felt as if she'd been punched in the stomach or slapped in the face. Or both.

She made it all the way to the outside courthouse steps before strong fingers closed around her upper arm, easily halting her.

"Hold on, Jen."

"No." But the protest was purely for show, because no way could she break Grady's hold.

"What's wrong? You won."

"Did I?"

"Yes. The judge gave me uncontested custody of the girls. It's over."

"Is it?"

"Would you quit asking questions," he said, exasperated.

"I haven't even started."

"Okay."

"Let me go."

"So you can take off again? I don't think so."

"How far can I get in these heels?" she asked, lifting one foot.

The intensity in his eyes as he looked at her nylon-clad ankle could have set fire to dry brush. Damn, she didn't need this right now. But he dropped his hand.

"How long have you known?" she asked.

"What?"

"That Jack had found enough to lock Billy up and throw away the key?"

"Not long."

"Did you know last night?"

He hesitated only a moment before nodding. "But, Jen—"

"So that's why you weren't worried. Why you were so cool."

"I had to keep it quiet. He could have run if word had gotten out."

"From me? You think I would've leaked something like that?"

"Of course not. Listen to me—"

"You don't have anything to say that I want to hear."

"I love you, Jen."

If she hadn't been so angry and profoundly hurt, the sincerity of his look might have penetrated. But she was furious. And so completely devastated that she needed to find a place not so profoundly public where she could cry her eyes out.

"I'm glad the girls are finally and completely yours. Give them each a kiss for me." Then she met Grady's gaze and filled her own with so much contempt she was sure he wouldn't see how she truly felt. "I never want to see you again."

Jen poked her head into the sheriff's office. No way did she want to be there. "Hi, Phoebe. You ready to go?"

"Hey, Jen." Phoebe Johnson looked up from where she sat at the buddy desk behind the counter. The attractive young deputy had called Jen's office a little while ago and suggested they have lunch together. Jen was eager to make friends in town, but not so eager to meet the woman on Grady's turf.

In the four days since court, he'd tried countless times and used numerous methods and technologies to communicate with her. The latest was an e-mail message, which she'd promptly deleted. With a flourish. Afterward, she'd said a silent thank-you to the computer god for the delete button.

Now she wished someone would invent a way she could move her office so it wasn't beside his. The pain of knowing he was just on the other side of the wall, but completely out of her reach, was almost more than she could bear. When Phoebe had invited her to lunch, she'd told Jen to come into the office when she was ready to go. Then had promptly hung up. Jen had almost called back. Then decided to be a grown-up, mature woman.

"You ready to go?" Jen repeated.

"Yeah. But when I told the sheriff we were going to lunch, he said he wanted to see you. Something about wrapping up paperwork on that whole custody thing."

Jen's heart pounded hard against her ribs. Just the mention of his name was enough to make her palms sweat, her knees weak and her pulse race. Which was truly unfortunate, since he was the last man she wanted to see—and the only man in the world she wanted. It just hurt too much knowing he could never trust her. Because that meant he couldn't love her. At least, not the way she loved him. Anything less was unacceptable.

When Zach died she'd lost the love of her life. Or so she'd thought. She hadn't believed she would ever fall in love again. Still, she'd found the courage to go on. And she'd fallen head over heels for Grady. Who was very much alive. Which made the situation all the more tragic, because they could have had something really wonderful. But she'd survived tragedy before; she could do it again.

"Tell the sheriff whatever it is we can discuss it over the phone."

The phone was safe. She could disconnect him. Almost as good as the delete button. Only, the best part of e-mail was that she didn't have to hear his deep, wonderful voice.

Phoebe stood and walked over to the counter. "He was pretty insistent that he see you."

Jen's heart pounded harder, making her wonder how much abuse her ticker could take. The temptation to see him tied her in knots. It had been four *whole* days since Billy Bob Adams had been led away in handcuffs and the threat to Grady's children had been eliminated. Four days since she'd told him she never wanted to see him again. But that hadn't discouraged Destiny's intrepid sheriff.

In spite of their insurmountable problems, his determination generated a tiny hopeful glow inside her. She'd missed him terribly in the past four days. Who was she kidding? She'd missed him terribly five minutes after she'd stormed away from him at the courthouse.

Phoebe walked to the end of the counter and angled her head toward the offices down the hall. "Come on, Jen. Just for a minute. Get it over with. Then we'll go have a nice lunch."

Jen didn't for one minute believe he had anything to say about the custody case. But the town wasn't big enough for the both of them. Sooner or later she would run into him. Might as well get it over with. Besides, it wasn't right to put Phoebe in the middle of this.

"Oh. All right."

Jen followed the other woman down the hall. Finally the deputy knocked on the door marked Sheriff.

"Come in." It was Grady's voice, all right, but with a healthy dose of grump thrown in.

Good. She was glad he was miserable. And since when had she become such a liar? She wanted to put her arms around him and take away his unhappiness. But that was a privilege she hadn't earned.

Phoebe poked her head in. "Jensen Stevens is here to see you, boss."

"Send her in."

Phoebe put her hand at Jen's back and gave her a good, solid nudge into the room. Behind his paper-cluttered desk, Grady stood. He looked good. Too good. He had no right to look that good when Jen knew she looked so bad. She hadn't slept well in days. The bags under her eyes would now hold enough for a trip around the world. Twice. At the deputy's urging, she walked over to the desk.

His expression shuttered. "Hi."

"Hi," she answered, not quite meeting his gaze. "You wanted to see me? Paperwork from the case?"

"I didn't ask to see you," he said, frowning. He walked around the desk to stand beside her.

They both turned to look at Phoebe, at the same time pointing at the deputy.

"We've been had," Jen said, meeting Grady's gaze for a moment.

In the blink of an eye Phoebe Johnson reached behind her back and whipped out the cuffs from her leather belt. She snapped them on Jen and Grady before they figured out what she was doing.

"Now," she said, looking from one to the other, "I'm tired of this nonsense. You can stay that way until you learn to play nice."

"I'm never going to lunch with you again," Jen said, tugging at the restraining bracelet.

"Phoebe, you're fired." Grady ground out the words.

The woman stood at the door and nodded. "Suits me fine. I don't want to work for a man with a bad attitude as big as Indiana and a brain the size of a pea. And don't even get me started on a woman who could out-stubborn a two-year-old."

Then she walked out and shut the door.

Jen looked at Grady. Grady looked at Jen.

She turned away from him and started to cross her arms over her chest. Unfortunately, his arm came, too—halfway around her. When he started to lift his other arm, as if to fold her against him, she lowered her wrist.

"Don't you have a key for these?" she snapped.

"They're not my cuffs," he said. Oddly enough, amusement laced his voice.

Annoyed, she shot him a look. "This isn't funny, Grady."

"Yeah, Jen. It is. Where's your sense of humor?"

"I guess I lost it at the hearing the other day. By the way, how are the girls doing?"

"Great. They want to come and see you."

"I'd like that. But don't change the subject."

"I wouldn't dream of it. But *you* changed the subject."

"What were we talking about?"

"Your missing sense of humor."

"Oh. Yes. And just for the record, it's not missing. I know exactly where I left it. In Judge Kellerman's courtroom where you betrayed me."

"I never deceived you."

"Then I'd like to know what *you* call failing to inform me, first chair of your legal team, of the fact that you and your buddy Jack Riley had compiled enough charges to put Billy Bob Adams away for a good long time. And even if he didn't go to jail, which he did, there was enough evidence that he's unfit to have a dog let alone his nieces."

She lifted her hand with every intention of poking him in the chest. But it was her bad luck that his left wrist, shackled to her right one, came along for the ride. And it was heavy. Because it was twice the size of hers. Because he was a man. And he was strong and masculine. And sexy. And handsome. And—

Darn it all. Phoebe was going to hear about this.

"What do you call *not* telling me all that, if not betrayal?"

He folded his arms over his chest, pulling her up close and personal. "I call it, at worst, doing the wrong thing for the right reason."

"What right reason could there possibly be?"

"You."

"Puhleeze, Grady. You made a fool of me."

He shook his head. "Not true."

"You never truly believed you would lose custody, did you?"

"I had a few doubts. And you were right when you said be prepared and don't take anything for granted. But no. I never really believed I'd lose the kids."

"Then why…"

"Because more and more it became clear to me that you needed to do this."

She was weakening, but not quite ready to let him off the hook. "That's still not a good enough reason to string me along."

"How about because I love you?"

The building blocks of her towering anger swayed precariously. If it toppled, she would have no reserves of resistance left. And she still didn't think he'd paid enough for what he'd put her through.

She worked up a really good glare and aimed it at him. "Saying that is just out-and-out mean. It's cruel and unusual punishment. To lead me to believe there's a chance for us when nothing could be further from the truth."

"You're wrong. And if you'd give *me* half a chance to prove I love you—"

"Love? Hah! You've sure got a funny way of showing it."

"Because I let you win?"

She put her hand on her hip—the hand without the cuffs, or his hand would be practically on her hip, too. Then where would she be? Unable to form a coherent thought. Which wasn't far from where she was at the moment. Because she could have sworn he'd said he let her win. And the way she felt—well, suffice it to say if that was winning, she'd rather be the world's biggest loser.

"What are you talking about? What did I win?"

"My custody case. In front of the judge, you got Billy to admit he didn't want the girls. Now there will never be any question of him raising them."

"There's no question of that, because he's going up the river for a very long time. He'll be lucky if they don't throw away the key." She frowned. "Speaking of keys—don't you have one for these things?" she asked again.

She held up her wrist and tugged his with it.

"Look, Jen, for some reason you got it into your head that you needed to make up for the past." He folded his arms over his chest, tugging her up against him. For the second time.

Their bodies touched from chest to thigh and the heat of him seeped through her clothes. The solid length of him sorely tempted her. More than anything she wanted to be in his arms. But not out of pity.

Looking into her eyes, he said, "You needed to win this case. On your own. Our future was riding on it. That's why I kept it to myself."

"I lost sleep over this case. It cost me blood, sweat and tears. You knew it was over the night before the hearing. You could have put me out of my misery. All you had to do was tell me what Jack had found."

"What if Jack hadn't found anything?"

"But he did."

"But if he hadn't. Then what?" His eyes narrowed on her. "What would I have done without you? You never gave me a chance to tell you. It was the fingerprints that did the trick. We were able to match them to a string of aliases.''

"You could have told me,'' she said stubbornly.

"I wanted you to beat him on your own turf. And you did that. In spades. I was so proud of you.'' He let out a long breath. "Now it's time for you to be proud of yourself. Jen, the sin was Zach's, not yours. To believe that, you needed to win this case. And you did. Now I rest my case.''

More than anything she wanted to believe he meant every word he'd said. Especially that he loved her. But being wrong hurt so much more than she'd ever thought it could. And she loved him. Even more because he'd understood in such a profound way what this case had meant to her.

"I don't know why you bother to deny it, Grady. The truth is obvious. You didn't trust me with your girls. Not really. Not completely.''

"Yes, I did. And I still do. I just did what any good lawman would do, what any father would do in my shoes. I arranged for backup.''

She sighed. "If that's the way you see it, then we have nothing more to say to each other. Now, where can we get a key for these blasted things?'' she asked, tugging on his arm.

"We've got a hell of a lot more to say,'' he growled. "For starters, when did you get to be such a coward?''

"Excuse me?''

"You love me. I know you do. And I also know it scares the hell out of you. So you're throwing up road-blocks as fast as you can. You're afraid.''

"Baloney.''

"Nope.'' He shook his head. "You're scared to

death of caring for someone. No matter what, you loved Zach. You learned early and hard how precarious life can be. And you're afraid to let yourself care again.''

"Don't be ridiculous.''

"Then tell me I'm wrong. Tell me you don't love me.'' He stared down at her—waiting.

She couldn't tell him he was wrong. Because he was so very right. She *was* afraid—very afraid. She loved Grady so much. The feelings were so much bigger than she'd had ten years ago. Meaning the hurt of losing him would be bigger, too. Surviving it was a challenge she didn't think she could handle.

"Oh, I get it,'' she said, bluffing. She had to tilt her head back to meet his gaze—she hoped with defiance shining in her eyes and not the complete and utter adoration she very much feared was there. She tapped the metal handcuff on his wrist. "This is some hostage negotiating tactic. I've got news for you, Sheriff— we're both hostages and you're negotiating with the wrong person.'' She glanced over her shoulder and cocked her thumb toward the door. "You should be working a deal with your deputy for the key to these blasted handcuffs.''

He shook his head. "Nope. I'm mediating with the absolute right person. I'm just using the wrong technique.''

His eyes took on an intensity that robbed her lungs of oxygen. He put his left hand at her waist, effectively trapping her right hand there, as well. Then he cupped her cheek and jaw in his right palm, tipping her face up. Lowering his head, he gently touched his mouth to hers.

At the first moment of contact, Jen knew she'd lost.

And she couldn't have been happier. She could meet him word for word until he cried "Uncle." But she couldn't fight this. He was showing her with his hands, his body, his mouth everything words weren't enough to say. He loved her. Not only that. He was eliciting from her what she couldn't hide: she loved him back.

When he lifted his lips from hers, she tasted reluctance. He looked deeply into her eyes, and in his own she saw hope and fear, but most of all love. With his hand still cupping her cheek, he said, "I love you, Jen. I never knew what love was until you. And I'll never know it again if you walk away. I swear on everything I hold dear that I will do everything in my power to always be here for you."

Tears filled her eyes and her lips trembled. "Grady, I..."

He shook his head. "Don't cry. Please don't. I couldn't stand that. The last thing I want to do is hurt you."

"I know. And you're right. I tried so hard not to have feelings for you."

Anticipation gleamed in his eyes. "Does that mean you do have feelings for me?"

She nodded and the tears welling in her eyes slid down her cheeks. "I couldn't help it."

"Say it," he said, his voice ragged. "Tell me."

"I love you, Grady O'Connor. But I'm afraid..."

"It's why they call it falling in love. It is scary. But you take a leap. Give it your best shot and grab all the happiness you can—while you can."

"All of a sudden, you sure got smart about love for a man who's never *been* in love."

"I didn't get smart all of a sudden. I've just been waiting for you."

She smiled. "You're just about the best man I've ever known. I would rather have whatever time fate gives me with you than a thousand years with anyone else."

He released his breath, and relief stood out in his eyes. His shoulders relaxed as tension drained away. He smiled, chasing the shadows from his handsome face. "Then there's only one more question I need to ask."

She held up their hands with the handcuffs still attached. "I think your interrogation methods are interesting."

He grinned. "Actually the method is Phoebe's, but remind me to give her a raise."

"You have to hire her back first. But you were going to ask me something."

"Since we're prisoners of love," he said, looking ruefully at their hardware-connected wrists, "let's make it legal. Will you marry me, Jen?"

"Yes," she said, sniffling as tears filled her eyes again. "Now I suggest we find a locksmith or a blacksmith or a hacksaw and get these things off. When a girl gets engaged, she expects jewelry, but not matching bracelets."

He tugged her with him to his desk and pulled a key out of the top drawer. In seconds, he'd freed them.

Rubbing her wrist, she said, "I smell a conspiracy."

"Nope. Phoebe took matters into her own hands, presumably because I've been unbearable for the last few days. But sooner or later I'd have made you listen. One way or the other, I never would have let you go."

"Better late than never," she agreed. "I guess some things are just meant to be. And it's just about impossible to resist a man in uniform."

Epilogue

Eighteen months later

Jen smiled up at Grady as he slipped his arm around her waist. Then she looked down at their sleeping four-month-old daughter in her arms. "Emma is going to be hungry soon," she whispered.

"Perfect timing. The ceremony is just about over," her husband answered.

Along with their friends and neighbors, they were gathered at Dev Hart's ranch to share in the wedding celebration of Polly Morgan and Frank Holloway. Hannah's mother and the town doctor had finally decided to tie the knot. They'd claimed the wait had been necessary in order to snag the spotlight. Between the epidemic of weddings and births in the past year and a half, it hadn't been easy.

Hannah had married Dev right after she'd turned down the offer in Los Angeles for a prestigious position in a pediatric practice. Now she was Frank's partner in the medical office and Dev's partner in life. Together they were raising Ben, his son from his first marriage. The boy was thriving with two parents who loved him. As Jen watched the three of them standing by as her mother took vows, Dev put his palm on Hannah's gently rounded belly. Another Hart would be here before long—a girl, according to the ultrasound.

Jen glanced to her right and smiled at her sister, Taylor. Her husband, Mitch Rafferty, held their baby son in his arms. They'd had a double wedding thirteen months ago and their babies had been born within days of each other. Rumor had it that often happened with sisters. Everyone had teased them about having more kids soon, and flip-flopping genders so they'd each have a boy and a girl. She figured that was probably going to happen. Although as the mother of twins now, Jen figured she would always be two ahead.

Then her gaze swung to the left, to Jack and Maggie Riley. Faith stood beside them and couldn't stop touching her baby brother's tiny feet. He was two months older than her own baby. After learning Faith was the daughter he'd never known about, Jack had jumped into fatherhood with the same focus he'd used to scour databases for the information to put Billy Bob Adams in jail where he could never hurt anyone again. After that, Jack and Maggie had married quickly and quietly and she'd gotten pregnant right away.

Jen's gaze settled on her own deputy Cupid—Phoebe Johnson. Standing on Grady's other side, the pretty young woman in a satin slip dress couldn't have looked less like law enforcement. But she was still after Grady's job, and her road was more uphill. The sheriff had retired and Grady had won a landslide victory in the special election to replace him. He was now Destiny's official sheriff.

As the bride and groom kissed and the crowd cheered, Jen looked up at Grady. "Do you think if Phoebe hadn't interfered we'd be together now?"

"Oh, yeah. It's destiny." He smiled. "But it might have taken a little longer, considering you're so stubborn."

"You silver-tongued devil," she teased. "I guess her crash course in communication did speed up the process."

"Think we can return the favor?" he asked, love shining in his eyes.

"You never know. This is Destiny." She rested her head against his shoulder. Since that day in his office when they'd been handcuffed together, she was so full of happiness it often bubbled over. When it did, her comment was always the same as now. "And this is what happens if we fall in love."

* * * * *

Don't miss the reprisal of Silhouette Romance's popular miniseries

When King Michael of Edenbourg goes missing, his devoted family and loyal subjects make it their mission to bring him home safely!

Their search begins March 2001 and continues through June 2001.

On sale March 2001: **THE EXPECTANT PRINCESS**
by bestselling author **Stella Bagwell** (SR #1504)

On sale April 2001: **THE BLACKSHEEP PRINCE'S BRIDE**
by rising star **Martha Shields** (SR #1510)

On sale May 2001: **CODE NAME: PRINCE**
by popular author **Valerie Parv** (SR #1516)

On sale June 2001: **AN OFFICER AND A PRINCESS**
by award-winning author **Carla Cassidy** (SR #1522)

Available at your favorite retail outlet.

Where love comes alive™

Visit Silhouette at www.eHarlequin.com   SRRW3

These New York Times *bestselling authors*
have created stories to capture the hearts and minds
of women everywhere.
Here are three classic tales about the power of love—
and the wonder of discovering the place
where you belong....

FINDING HOME

DUNCAN'S BRIDE
by
LINDA HOWARD

CHAIN LIGHTNING
by
ELIZABETH LOWELL

POPCORN AND KISSES
by
KASEY MICHAELS

Available only from Silhouette
at your favorite retail outlet.

Silhouette®

Where love comes alive™

Visit Silhouette at www.eHarlequin.com   PSFH

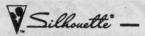

Silhouette®

where love comes alive—online...

eHARLEQUIN.com

your romantic magazine

—Indulgences—

♥ Monthly guides to indulging yourself,
such as:
★ Tub Time: A guide for bathing beauties
★ Magic Massages: A treat for tired feet

—Horoscopes—

♥ Find your daily Passionscope, weekly
Lovescopes and Erotiscopes

♥ Try our compatibility game

—Romantic Movies—

♥ Read all the latest romantic
movie reviews

—Royal Romance—

♥ Get the latest scoop on your favorite
royal romances

—Romantic Travel—

♥ For the most romantic destinations, hotels
and travel activities

All this and more available at
www.eHarlequin.com

SINTE1R2

If you enjoyed what you just read,
then we've got an offer you can't resist!

Take 2 bestselling love stories FREE!

Plus get a FREE surprise gift!

Clip this page and mail it to Silhouette Reader Service™

IN U.S.A.	IN CANADA
3010 Walden Ave.	P.O. Box 609
P.O. Box 1867	Fort Erie, Ontario
Buffalo, N.Y. 14240-1867	L2A 5X3

YES! Please send me 2 free Silhouette Romance® novels and my free surprise gift. After receiving them, if I don't wish to receive anymore, I can return the shipping statement marked cancel. If I don't cancel, I will receive 6 brand-new novels every month, before they're available in stores! In the U.S.A., bill me at the bargain price of $3.15 plus 25¢ shipping and handling per book and applicable sales tax, if any*. In Canada, bill me at the bargain price of $3.50 plus 25¢ shipping and handling per book and applicable taxes**. That's the complete price and a savings of at least 10% off the cover prices—what a great deal! I understand that accepting the 2 free books and gift places me under no obligation ever to buy any books. I can always return a shipment and cancel at any time. Even if I never buy another book from Silhouette, the 2 free books and gift are mine to keep forever.

215 SEN DFNQ
315 SEN DFNR

Name	(PLEASE PRINT)	
Address	Apt.#	
City	State/Prov.	Zip/Postal Code

* Terms and prices subject to change without notice. Sales tax applicable in N.Y.
** Canadian residents will be charged applicable provincial taxes and GST.
All orders subject to approval. Offer limited to one per household and not valid to current Silhouette Romance® subscribers.
® are registered trademarks of Harlequin Enterprises Limited.

SROM01   ©1998 Harlequin Enterprises Limited

BESTSELLING AUTHORS

Linda Lael Miller
Kasey Michaels
Barbara Delinsky &
Diana Palmer

Lead

TAKE5

Covering everything from tender love to
sizzling passion, there's a TAKE 5 volume for
every type of romance reader.

PLUS

With two proofs-of-purchase
from any two Take 5
volumes you can receive
THE ART OF ROMANCE
absolutely free!
(see inside a volume of
TAKE 5 for details)

AND

With $5.00 worth of coupons inside each volume,
this is one deal you shouldn't miss!

Look for it in March 2002.

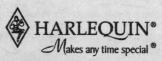

Visit us at www.eHarlequin.com

TAKE5POP

Silhouette Romance introduces tales of
enchanted love and things beyond explanation
in the new series

Soulmates

Couples destined for each other are brought
together by the powerful magic of love....

A precious gift brings
A HUSBAND IN HER EYES
by Karen Rose Smith (on sale March 2002)

Dreams come true in
CASSIE'S COWBOY
by Diane Pershing (on sale April 2002)

A legacy of love arrives
BECAUSE OF THE RING
by Stella Bagwell (on sale May 2002)

*Available at
your favorite retail outlet.*

Silhouette®
Where love comes alive™

Visit Silhouette at www.eHarlequin.com
SRSOUL